HAPPY ENDINGS

Edited and Compiled by
Gerald Downey

This book is dedicated to Ellen, Kelly and Kevin, who put up with my strange sense of humor every day.

INTRODUCTION

Almost as long as people have been around, they have loved stories. Anecdotes. Tales. Of course, I'm assuming a lot because I haven't been around as long as the entire human race. But I couldn't think of a better way to introduce this collection.

Some of the stories people like best are jokes. This is evidenced by the fact that, ever since ancient man fired up the first kerosene-powered computer and sent the first email, folks have spent an inordinate amount of time – usually time they should be spending working – sending each other jokes.

For the past decade, I've casually collected bits and pieces of jokes and funny stories sent to me by friends, or told to me as I stumbled through life as a writer and producer of ads and commercials. I managed to save many of them in files marked *Funny Stuff*. And now, I've taken what I consider to be the best of these, and I've turned them into little stories, each of which should take no more than a minute or two to read, and each of which has one thing in common: an ending that will make you smile. A Happy Ending. OK, so I didn't spend a lot of sleepless nights thinking of a name for this collection. What can I say? Hit me with a brick.

Anyway, whether you've heard these little stories before, or are reading them now for the first time, I hope they'll bring a smile to your face and some happiness into your life. Maybe you'll even laugh out loud at some of them, as I did.

Enjoy!

Jerry Downey

Contents

ONE NIGHT AT THE IRISH PUB 1

THE AMAZING CLAUDE 3

THE COMPOSER 5

THE NIGHT OF THE TREES 7

SUNDAY MORNINGS WITH GRANDPA 9

A REMARKABLE FAMILY TRADITION 11

THE NEW SALES GUY 13

THE NEW LIE DETECTOR 15

AN ELEPHANT NEVER FORGETS 17

OLD TIMERS' BAR 19

POTTY MOUTHS 21

THE MAGICAL SILVER WALLS 23

THE IRISH BANK ROBBERY 25

CHECKING IN, CHECKING OUT 27

THE POKER GAME 29

MEDICAL MIX-UP 31

THE HELICOPTER RIDE 33

THREE ELDERLY SISTERS 35

OLD FRIENDS 37

HEALTH SCARE 39

MAMA'S GIFTS 41

JEFF AND MOLLY 43

MEMORIES 45

THE MOOSE HUNTERS 47

LATE ARRIVAL 49

THE SENSITIVE MAN 51

RADICAL PROCEDURE 53

ONE NIGHT AT THE FARM 55

THE ENCOUNTER 57

THE AMAZING ARMAND 59

BOBBY AND BILLY 61

BEING NEIGHBORLY 63

POLISH SAUSAGE 65

NO BABY TALK! 67

SOLITUDE 69

BIG HELP 71

HEALTHY LIFESTYLE 73

PLAYING THROUGH 75

BEAR FACTS 77

THE BIG DECISION 79

HOTEL BILL 81

THE MAN AND THE MOUSE 83

AN OLD WESTERN TALE 85

ANOTHER OLD WESTERN TALE 87

SATURDAY AT THE BARBERSHOP 89

THE LUCKY IRISH GOLFER 91

CHEAP MOTEL 93

HIS DYING WISH 95

WORKING HOMICIDE 97

HOW SOW-EET IT IS! 99

GAS AND SEX 101

CONFESSION 103

KILLER LUNCH 105

A MAN AND HIS CAT 107

BAD DOG! 109

BENEVOLENT BARBER 111

GOLF – WITH AN ATTITUDE 113

BOBBY AND JOLENE 115

MY VISIT WITH GRAMPS 117

DON AND MARGE 119

UNEMPLOYMENT ISN'T WORKING 121

AT THE PEARLY GATES 123

GROOVY DATE 125

FEELING FINE 127

THE BLONDE AND THE PEST 129

GORILLA ON THE ROOF 131

GRANDMA'S BOYFRIEND 133

PERFECT FIT 135

HUNGRY MONKEY 137

STOPPED FOR SPEEDING 139

THE PARROT 141

JOB QUALIFICATIONS 143

FUSSIN' AN' A-FEUDIN' 145

LUCK OF THE IRISH 147

ALL ABOARD! 149

ROUGH NIGHT 151

THE BOY IN THE CLOSET 153

AMAZING MEDICINE 155

THE WORLD'S BEST HUSBAND 157

PATIENT PATIENT 159

SUNDAY SCHOOL 161

SHIRLEY 163

TRAVELING WITH THE POPE 165

MARBLE RYE 167

CONSEQUENCES 169

CHINESE NEWLYWEDS 171

WORLD'S FASTEST GOAT 173

ONE LAST FLING 175

MURPHY'S LATE ARRIVAL 177

SHARING 179

THE HORTH WHITHPERER 181

THE PICKLE SLICER INCIDENT 183

ELLEN'S VACATION IN ROME 185

RAISIN BREAD 187

BIRTHDAY WISH 189

LIFE IN THE HILLS 191

AN IRISH LAD'S CONFESSION 193

SPEED TRAP 195

THE OLD MAN AND THE KEYS 197

ORIGINAL EQUIPMENT 199

WHAT ARE FRIENDS FOR? 201

LIKE IT WAS YESTERDAY 203

THE THREE BARS 205

JESUS IS WATCHING! 207

HAUL PASS 209

THE WAGER 211

BLUE BLOOD VS. BLUE COLLAR 213

TOUGH GUY 215

FITTING PUNISHMENT 217

HAM SANDWICH 219

THE PUZZLE 221

MAFIA BOOKKEEPER 223

ALL ABOARD! 225

EFFICIENCY 227

HIS FINAL HOURS 229

GHOST CAR 231

SEX AFTER DEATH? 233

ONE SMART DOG 235

ANOTHER SMART DOG 237

ITALIAN HONEYMOON 239

THE BAR BET 241

THE CABBIE AND THE NUN 243

THE ITALIAN FIREFIGHTERS 245

A TOUCHING LOVE STORY 247

CHRISTMAS IN HEAVEN 249

LITTLE RED RIDING HOOD 251

PEANUTS 253

WHERE ARE WE? 255

SAY WHAT? 257

THE MARRIAGE COUNSELOR 259

CHANCE MEETING 261

THREE OLD GUYS 263

LUNCHTIME RELIGION 265

PULLING A PRANK ON GRAMPS 267

WHAT'S IN A NAME? 269

ONE NIGHT AT THE IRISH PUB

THE MEN SAT side-by-side at the bar of the Blarney Stone pub. It was late in the evening, and they had been there quite awhile. Finally, one guy turned to the other and, with a heavy Irish brogue, said, "I've been listening to ya and can't help but notice that you're from Ireland."

The other guy said, in an equally heavy brogue, "Ah, right you are m'lad!"

The first guy said, "I'm from the Emerald Isle meself! So, then, what town would you be comin' from?"

The other guy said, "Born an' raised in Dublin, I was."

"So am I! Faith and begorrah! And what street did you live on in Dublin?"

"I grew up on McCleary Street. A lovely little area it was, on the west end of town."

The first guy said, "Sure an' it's a small world. 'Tis the same neighborhood where I grew up! And to what school would you have been going?"

The other guy answered, "Well now, I went to St. Mary's, of course."

Excitedly, the first guy said, "So did I! Tell me, what was yer mother's name?"

The other guy answered, "Ah, me sainted mother's name was Margaret."

The first guy exclaimed, "Lord above, I can hardly believe our good fortune at winding up in the same pub tonight. Can you believe it? Me *own* sainted mother was named Margaret!"

About this time, another regular patron of the bar walked in, sat down, and said to the bartender, "Hey, Mike! What's new?"

Shaking his head, the bartender walked over and muttered,

"Aaah, nothin' much, but it's gonna be a long night tonight."

The customer asked, "Why's that?"

The bartender nodded toward the two Irishmen and said, "The Murphy twins are drunk again!"

THE AMAZING CLAUDE

IT WAS ENTERTAINMENT night at the senior center. An excited buzz ran through the crowd because The Amazing Claude was topping the bill. Seniors were bused in from miles around to see the famed hypnotist do his stuff. It was a much-anticipated event.

As Claude went to the front of the meeting room, he announced, "Unlike most hypnotists who invite two or three people to the stage and put them in a trance, I intend to hypnotize each and every member of the audience."

The excitement was electric as Claude reached into his coat and withdrew a beautiful antique pocket watch. He instructed the audience, "I want each of you to keep your eye on this antique watch. It is a very special watch. It has been in my family for six generations."

The Amazing Claude then began to swing the watch gently back and forth, while quietly chanting, "Watch the watch. Watch the watch. Watch the watch."

The crowd of seniors became mesmerized as the watch swayed back and forth, light gleaming off its polished surface. Hundreds of pairs of eyes followed the swinging watch until, suddenly, it slipped from the hypnotist's fingers and fell to the floor, breaking into a hundred pieces.

"*Shit!*" shouted the Hypnotist.

It took three days to clean up the senior center.

THE COMPOSER

THE ECONOMY WAS terrible, and the talented, famous music composer just couldn't find a job. Finally, exasperated and desperate for work, he took a job in the San Fernando Valley, just north of Hollywood, writing the musical score for a porno movie.

Despite the nature of the movie, he decided to give it his best effort. While most XXX-rated films featured a throbbing bass, an occasional saxophone, and a repetitive beat, he wrote a masterpiece – what, he was sure, would be considered the finest score to ever grace a pornographic film.

A few months later, he was walking past a XXX theatre, and on the marquee he saw the name of the movie for which he had written the music. Because his was a recognizable face, the composer ran home and put on a trench coat and hat so that no one would recognize him. Then, he went back to the theatre and watched the movie.

It was pretty raunchy – worse than his worst expectations. Women were doing it with men in every conceivable position. Men were doing it with men. Women with women. Old people. Young people. Couples and groups. Women with dogs. And so forth. But under all this obscene filth and nastiness, there was a beautiful, glorious musical score.

The composer was devastated. Anxious to know whether anyone even cared about the music in the movie, he looked around and spotted a middle-aged couple in the next row. As the movie was nearing its end, the composer leaned over to the couple and said, "Isn't the music beautiful?"

The couple looked at him and said, "Music, hell! We just came to see our dog!"

Happy Endings

THE NIGHT OF THE TREES

PADDY WAS A hard-drinking Irishman who, too often, took the dangerous risk of driving home after an evening of drinking, and this night was one of those nights.

Paddy was driving home after downing a few too many pints at the local pub.

As he turned a corner, much to his horror, he saw a tree in the middle of the road! Thinking as quickly as his condition would allow, he swerved to avoid it. Almost too late, he realized there was another tree, directly in his path! He swerved again and discovered that, somehow, he must have driven off the road because his route home suddenly became a veritable slalom course! He swerved and veered madly from side to side to avoid the trees.

Moments later, Paddy heard a police siren and brought his car to a stop. He closed his eyes and sat back with a sigh of relief as the police officer approached his car.

The constable said, "What on earth are ye doin', Paddy me boy? Why are ye swervin' from side to side? Sure an' you'll kill yerself!"

Paddy took a deep breath and began to tell the policeman about all the trees in the road when the constable stopped him in mid-sentence and said, "Fer cryin' out loud, ya damn fool! That's yer air freshener!"

Happy Endings

SUNDAY MORNINGS WITH GRANDPA

UPON HEARING THAT her elderly grandfather had just passed away, Katie went straight to her grandparents' house to visit her 95-year-old grandmother and comfort her.

When she asked how her grandpa had died, her grandmother replied, "He had a heart attack while we were making love on Sunday morning."

Katie was taken aback by her grandmother's frankness and shocked that her grandparents were having sex at such an advanced age. She told her grandmother that two people nearly 100 years old having sex was surely asking for trouble. Certainly, Grandpa's death proved her concern was realistic.

"Oh no, my dear," replied granny. "Many years ago, realizing our advanced age, we determined that the best time to do it was on Sunday mornings when the bells from nearby St. John's church were ringing. It was lovely. Just the right rhythm: nice and slow and even. Nothing too strenuous. Simply in on the Ding and out on the Dong."

Grandma paused to wipe away a tear with a delicate, lavender scented handkerchief, and continued, "He'd still be alive today if that damned ice cream truck hadn't come along!"

Happy Endings

A REMARKABLE FAMILY TRADITION

GROWING UP IN the hills of West Virginia, Bobby had long heard stories of a remarkable and mysterious family tradition. It seems that his father, grandfather, and great-grandfather, defying the laws of nature, all had been able to walk on water on their 18th birthday! On that special day, each of them walked across Bug Lake to the saloon on the far side and enjoyed their first legal drink.

So, Bobby's 18th birthday finally arrived. Now it was his turn to adopt this mysterious family tradition and follow in the footsteps of his male ancestors. He couldn't wait.

Bobby and his friend Cletus took a boat out to the middle of Bug Lake. Bobby took a big, nervous breath, climbed out of the boat – and nearly drowned. Using an oar, Cletus barely managed to pull Bobby to safety. They returned to shore and, furious and confused, Bobby went to see his grandmother.

"Granny," said Bobby, "It's mah 18th birthday. So why cain't I walk 'cross Bug Lake to the saloon, like Pa, and his Pa, and his Pa before him?"

Granny looked deeply into Bobby's troubled brown eyes and said, "Because your Pa, your Grampa, and your great Grampa all was born in February when the lake is hard-frozen, and you was born in August, ya dumb-ass!"

THE NEW SALES GUY

AFTER LOSING HIS job as a salesman as a sporting goods store in Mississippi, a young guy moved to Florida and looked for another job. He went to a big box, "everything under one roof" warehouse store where members could buy anything, from food to refrigerators, clothing to cars.

The manager said, "Do you have any sales experience?"

The young man, who stuttered a bit, said, "Y-yes, I was a s-salesman back in M-Mississippi, b-but they fired me c-cuz I stutter."

Well, the manager liked the kid, so he gave him a job. "You start tomorrow. I'll come down after closing time, and we'll see how you did."

The first day was rough, but the young man got through it. After the store was locked up, the boss came down and asked, "How many customers bought something from you today?"

The kid said, "W-w...One."

The boss said, "Just one? Our salespeople average 20 to 30 customers a day, sometimes more. How much was the sale for?"

The kid said, "$132,467.59"

The boss said, "$132, 467.59? What on earth did you sell?"

The kid said, "W-well, f-first I sold him a s-small fish hook. Then a m-medium fish hook. Th-then a larger fish hook. Th-then I sold him a new r-rod and reel, and fishing g-gear. Then, I asked him wh-where he was goin' fishin', and he s-said down the coast. S-so I told him he was g-gonna need a b-boat. S-so we w-went down to the B-boat Department, and I s-sold him a 22 f-foot, twin engine C-Chris Craft. Then h-he said he didn't think his Toyota Co-corolla could pull it, so I t-took him down to the Automotive D-department and sold him th-that 4x4 F-Ford Expedition."

The boss said, "A guy came in here to buy a fish hook and you sold him fishing gear, a *boat* and a *truck*?"

The kid said, "N-no, sir. The g-guy came in here to buy t-tampons for his wife, and I said, 'D-dude, your w-weekend's sh-shot. Y'all might as well j-just go fishin'!'"

THE NEW LIE DETECTOR

JOHN WAS A salesman's delight when it came to any kind of new and unusual gimmick. His wife, Marsha, had long ago given up trying to get him to change. One day, John came home with another of his unusual purchases. It was a robot that, John claimed, was actually a lie detector.

It was about 5:30 that afternoon when Tommy, their 13-year old son, came home from school. Tommy was over two hours late.

"Where have you been, Tommy?" asked John. "Why are you more than two hours late getting home?"

"Several of us went to the library to work on an extra credit project," said Tommy.

Suddenly, the robot walked around the table and slapped Tommy, knocking him completely out of his chair.

"Son," said John, "this robot is a lie detector. Now, tell us where you really were after school."

"We went to Bobby's house and watched a movie," Tommy confessed.

"What did you watch?" asked Marsha.

"The Ten Commandments," answered Tommy.

The robot went around to Tommy and slapped him, once again knocking him off his chair.

With tears in his eyes and lip quivering, Tommy got up, sat down and said, "I'm sorry I lied. We were really watching an X-rated movie."

"I'm ashamed of you, son," said John. "When I was your age, I never lied to my parents."

The robot then walked around to John and gave him a whack that nearly knocked him out of his chair.

Marsha doubled over in laughter. On the verge of tears, she said, "Boy, did you ever ask for *that* one, John! You can't be too mad at Tommy for lying. After all, he is your son!"

With that, the robot immediately walked around to Marsha and knocked her out of her chair.

AN ELEPHANT NEVER FORGETS

ALL TOO OFTEN, we don't give animals credit for being as intelligent as many of them are. In 1986, Tom Spencer was on vacation in Kenya after graduating from Northwestern University.

On a hike through the bush, he came across a young bull elephant standing with one leg raised in the air. The elephant seemed distressed, so Tom approached it very carefully.

He got down on one knee, inspected the elephant's foot, and found a large piece of wood deeply embedded in it. As carefully and as gently as he could, Tom worked the wood out with his knife after which the elephant gingerly put down its foot. The elephant turned to face the man and, with a rather curious look on its face, stared at him for several tense moments. Tom stood frozen, thinking of nothing else but being trampled. Eventually, the elephant trumpeted loudly, turned, and walked away. Tom never forgot that elephant or the events of that day.

Twenty years later, Tom was walking through the Chicago Zoo with his teenage son. As they approached the elephant enclosure, one of the creatures turned and walked over to near where Tom and his son were standing. The large bull elephant stared at Tom, lifted its front foot off the ground, and then put it down. The elephant did that several times then trumpeted loudly, all the while staring at the man.

Remembering the encounter in 1986, Tom could not help but wonder if this was the same elephant. He summoned up his courage, climbed over the railing, and made his way into the enclosure. He walked right up to the elephant and stared back in wonder.

The elephant trumpeted again, wrapped its trunk around one of Tom's legs and slammed him against the railing, killing him instantly.

It was a different elephant.

Happy Endings

OLD TIMERS' BAR

FOUR RETIRED GUYS were walking down one of the quieter streets in Key West when they turned a corner and saw a saloon called Old Timers' Bar. On the window was a big sign that said "All Drinks 10¢." They looked at each other and went in, thinking, "This is too good to be true!"

A friendly old bartender welcomed them, saying, "Come on in, boys, and let me pour one for ya. What'll it be, gentlemen?"

The bar was fully stocked, so each of the men ordered a martini. In no time, the bartender served up four perfect martinis, and said, "That'll be 10¢ each, please."

The four guys stared at the bartender for a moment then looked at each other, thinking they were dreaming. They paid the 40¢, finished their martinis, and ordered another round.

Again, four excellent martinis were produced, and the bartender collected another 40¢.

Finally, curiosity got the best of the four guys, and one of them said to the bartender, "We've each had two perfect martinis and haven't even spent a dollar yet. How can you afford to serve drinks as good as these for a dime apiece?"

The bartender answered, "I'm a retired auto worker from Detroit, and I always wanted to own a bar. Last year, I won $150 million in the lottery, and decided to open this place. I don't need the money, but I can't give away liquor for free, so every drink costs a dime. Liquor, beer, wine, it all costs the same!"

"Wow! That's some story," one of the men said, and they ordered a third round.

While they were drinking, the men looked around and spotted six other patrons at the end of the bar. None of the six had drinks in front of them, and it appeared that they hadn't ordered anything the whole time they'd been there.

One of the men gestured toward the six customers at the end of the bar, and said, "What's with them?"

The bartender said, "Oh, they're retired folks, living here in South Florida. They're waiting for Happy Hour when drinks are half-price!"

POTTY MOUTHS

THE TWO BOYS, a seven-year-old and his five-year-old brother, were playing in their upstairs bedroom when Johnny, the seven-year-old, said, "You know what, Billy? I think it's about time we started cussing. Some of the boys at school do it, and the other kids think they're pretty cool."

The 5-year-old, not really knowing what Johnny was talking about but wanting to stay in his big brother's good graces, nodded his head in approval. That encouraged Johnny to continue with a mischievous look on his face: "When we go downstairs for breakfast, I'm gonna say something with the word 'hell' in it, and you say something with – let's see – the word 'ass' in it. Then, Mom will know we're big boys now."

Billy nodded again and agreed with enthusiasm.

When Mom walked into the kitchen, she asked Johnny what he wanted for breakfast. He replied, "Aw, hell, Mom. I guess I'll just have some Cheerios."

WHACK! You could hear Mom slap Johnny a block away. He flew out of his chair, tumbled across the kitchen floor, and stumbled upstairs, screaming and crying his eyes out with his mother in hot pursuit, slapping his rear with every step. She locked him in his room and said, "You will stay in that room until I let you out!"

Mom came back downstairs, looked at the 5-year-old and said, "And what do YOU want for breakfast, young man?"

"I don't know," Billy blubbered, "but you can bet your ass it won't be Cheerios!"

THE MAGICAL SILVER WALLS

A COUNTRY BOY and his daddy found themselves in a shopping center for the first time. Naturally, having lived deep in the hills their entire lives, they were amazed by almost everything they saw at the beautiful, new mall. But there was one thing that especially intrigued the boy and his dad: in the center of the mall, there were two shiny, silver walls that mysteriously moved apart and then slid back together again. When the shiny walls moved apart, people would often walk past them.

The boy asked, "Hey, Pa, what's 'at?"

And Daddy, never having seen an elevator before, responded, "Son, I jest don't know. I ain't never seen nuthin' like this in all my born days. I ain't got no idear whut it is."

While the boy and his daddy watched with amazement, a fat, old lady in a wheelchair rolled up to the silver walls and pressed a button. Soon, the walls opened, and the woman rolled between them into a small room. The walls closed and, as the country boy and his dad watched, small, circular numbers above the walls lit up sequentially.

They watched until the highest number was reached, and then the numbers began to light up in the reverse order. Finally, the silver walls opened again, and a beautiful blonde, who appeared to be in her mid-20s, stepped out.

Without taking his eyes off the young woman, the father turned to his son, leaned over, and quietly said, "Boy, go git yer mama!"

THE IRISH BANK ROBBERY

A<small>N ARMED, HOODED</small> robber burst into a branch of the Bank of Ireland one afternoon and announced a holdup. He ordered the tellers to load a sack full of cash while the few patrons who were in the bank at the time were forced to stand in place with their hands up over their heads.

As the thief was on his way out the door with his loot, one brave and foolish young man reached out and snatched the hood off the robber's head, revealing the thief's face. Not wanting to be identified, the robber shot the customer without hesitation.

The thief quickly looked around at the other customers and tellers, to see if anyone else had seen him. One of the tellers was looking straight at him, so he immediately shot her too.

By now, everyone in the bank was frightened and looking down at the floor, and the robber shouted, "Did anyone else see my face?"

After a moment of silence, an elderly Irish gent tentatively waved his hand and said, "I think me wife may have caught a glimpse…"

Happy Endings

CHECKING IN, CHECKING OUT

A COUPLE WHO lived in Chicago were embarking on their annual mid-winter vacation to Palm Beach. He left town on their planned departure date, but his wife was on a business trip and planned to meet him in Florida the next day.

When he reached their hotel in Palm Beach, the husband decided to send his wife a quick email to tell her he'd arrived safely. Unfortunately, he had a difficult time remembering his wife's office email address, and when he typed it from memory he transposed a couple of letters. So, instead of his note reaching his wife, it went to an elderly preacher's wife whose husband had passed away only the day before.

When the grieving widow read her email, she let out a scream and fell to the floor, dead.

Hearing her scream, the old woman's family rushed into her room and saw this note on the computer screen:

Dearest Wife,

Just got checked in. Everything is ready for your arrival tomorrow.

Your Loving Husband

PS: It sure is hot down here!

Happy Endings

THE POKER GAME

SIX RETIRED IRISHMEN were playing their weekly poker game in O'Brien's apartment. It was late in the evening when Paddy Murphy, who already had lost an unprecedented $500 that night, suddenly clutched his chest, gasped, and dropped dead of a heart attack, right at the table. Out of respect for their fallen brother, the other five finished the hand standing up.

Then, Michael O'Conner looked around and said, "Well, boys, someone's gotta tell ol' Paddy's wife that her husband's dead. Who will it be?"

None of them wanted that awkward task, particularly since they'd been drinking all night, so they drew straws, and Kevin Gallagher drew the short straw.

O'Brien said, "Now Kevin, when you're talking to Mrs. Murphy, be discreet, be gentle, and don't make a bad situation even worse than it is."

"Don't you worry, boys," said Gallagher, "I'm the most discreet Irishman you'll ever meet. Why, discretion is me middle name! Just leave it to me!" And off he went.

Arriving at Murphy's house, Gallagher knocked on the door. Mrs. Murphy answered and said, angrily, "What'll *you* be wantin' at this hour, Gallagher? Where's me husband?"

Gallagher said, "Evenin', Mrs. Murphy. I've got some bad news. Your Paddy lost $500 in the poker game tonight and is afraid to come home."

Furious, Mrs. Murphy said, "You just tell him he can drop dead!"

"Sure an' I'll be goin' back and tellin' him, right away," said Gallagher. And he left.

MEDICAL MIX-UP

Mrs. Johnson went to the doctor's office to get her husband's test results.

The doctor said, "I'm sorry, Mrs. Johnson, but there has been a bit of a mix-up with your husband's tests, and we have a problem. Seems that when we sent your husband's samples to the lab, the samples from another Mr. Johnson were sent to them as well, and now we're uncertain as to which lab results are your husband's. Frankly, it's either bad news or terrible news."

What do you mean, bad news or terrible news?" said Mrs. Johnson.

Well, one Mr. Johnson tested positive for Alzheimer's, and the other tested positive for AIDS. We can't tell which test was your husband's test," said the doctor.

"That's awful," said Mrs. Johnson. "Can we do the test again?"

"Normally yes, but your particular health care coverage won't pay for these expensive tests more than once," said the doctor.

"Then, what am I supposed to do?" said Mrs. Johnson.

"Well, your health care company recommends that you drop your husband off in the middle of town. If he finds his way home, don't sleep with him!"

Happy Endings

THE HELICOPTER RIDE

ORRIS AND HIS wife Esther went to the state fair every year. And, every year, Morris would say, "Esther, I'd like to ride in that helicopter."

Esther always replied, "I know, Morris, but that helicopter ride costs fifty dollars, and fifty dollars is fifty dollars."

Then, one year, Esther and Morris went to the fair, and Morris said, "Esther, I'm 85 years old. If I don't ride in that helicopter, I might never get another chance." But, to this, Esther again replied, "Morris, that helicopter ride is fifty dollars. And fifty dollars is fifty dollars."

The pilot overheard their bickering, and said, "Folks, I'll make you a deal. I'll take both of you for a ride. If you can stop that bickering and stay quiet for the entire ride, I won't charge you for the ride. But if you say one word, it's fifty dollars."

Morris and Esther agreed, and up they went. The pilot did all sorts of fancy maneuvers for Morris, who had waited so long for a helicopter ride.

The pilot even did some daredevil tricks over and over again. And, throughout the ride, not a word was heard from Morris or Esther.

When they landed, the pilot said to Morris, "By golly, I did everything I could to get you to yell out, but you didn't. I'm impressed!"

Morris replied, "Well, to tell you the truth, I almost said something when Esther fell out, but you know, fifty dollars is fifty dollars."

THREE ELDERLY SISTERS

THE THREE ELDERLY sisters lived together in their own home for many years. Although they were getting up in years – they were 92, 94, and 96 years old, respectively – together they were able to manage independent living quite well, thank you.

One night, the 96-year-old sister drew a bath and, just as she was stepping into the tub, she paused and shouted to her sisters downstairs, "Was I getting into or out of the bath?"

Her 94-year-old sister shouted back, "I don't know, but hold on; I'll come upstairs and see!" She slowly started up the stairs and, halfway up, she paused and called out, "Was I going up the stairs or down?"

The comparatively young 92-year-old sister was sitting at the kitchen table, enjoying a cup of tea, when she heard all of the commotion her sisters were making. She smiled and shook her head, saying, "I sure hope I never get as forgetful as those two!" And, just for good measure, she knocked on the wooden tabletop.

She then yelled, "Don't worry, girls, I'll come up and help both of you as soon as I see who's at the door!"

OLD FRIENDS

TWO ELDERLY LADIES had been friends for decades. Over the years, they shared countless activities and adventures. Lately, one of their favorite activities was a weekly bridge game with friends.

One day, as they were playing cards, Mildred looked over at Gladys and said, "Now, don't get mad at me. I know we've been friends for years, but I seem to be drawing a blank. For the life of me, I just can't recall your name. I've thought and thought all evening, but I don't remember it. Please tell me what your name is, dear."

Gladys just sat and glared at her. For at least three minutes, she just stared and glared at Mildred. Finally, she said, "How soon do you need to know?"

Later, Mildred and Gladys were driving home with Mildred behind the wheel. Both of them could barely see over the dashboard, but Gladys was quite sure that Mildred had just gone through a red light.

A few moments later, they ran another red light. "I must be losing it," Gladys said to herself, "I could have sworn we just ran through another red light." She was getting nervous.

At the next intersection, sure enough, they ran through a third red light. Gladys turned to her friend and said, "Mildred, do you realize that we just ran through three red lights in a row? You could have killed us both!"

Mildred turned to Gladys and said, "Crap! Am I driving?"

Happy Endings

HEALTH SCARE

M̲RS. WHEELER WENT to the clinic where she was seen by one of the young doctors. After about five minutes in the examination room, she burst out of the room screaming and ran down the hall.

Mrs. Wheeler was intercepted by one of the older doctors, who calmed her down and asked her what the problem was. She told the doctor what had happened.

After listening to Mrs. Wheeler's story, the doctor was angry. He told Mrs. Wheeler to sit down and relax in another examination room then he marched back to where the young doctor who examined Mrs. Wheeler was writing on his clipboard.

"What's the matter with you?" the older doctor demanded. "Mrs. Wheeler is 62 years old, has four grown children and five grandchildren, and you told her she was pregnant?"

The young doctor continued writing on his clipboard and, without looking up, asked, "Does she still have the hiccups?"

MAMA'S GIFTS

$\mathbf{M}$AMA PUT HER four sons through college and made sure they studied. Two became prosperous doctors; two became successful lawyers, and now that she was in her twilight years, they decided to make this Christmas extra special by giving her extravagant gifts. The four brothers met over dinner one day and talked about what they gave Mama.

Barry said, "I bought Mama that big house in Palm Beach, where she can be comfortable."

Gary said, "And, as you know, I had a hundred thousand dollar home theatre built into her house."

Larry said, "I bought Mama a top-of-the-line Bentley, so she can get wherever she needs to go, in style."

And Harry said, "Well, guys, you know how Mama always loved reading the Bible, but she can't see very well, now, and her eyes get tired quickly. Anyway, I found an animal trainer in South Florida who spent five years training a parrot to memorize and recite the entire Bible! All Mama has to do is name the chapter and verse, and the parrot will recite it. It cost me $250,000, but I think it's well worth it."

The brothers were amazed and impressed when Harry described his unusual gift.

After the Holidays, Mama sent Thank You notes to each of the boys. She wrote:

Barry, the house you bought me is so huge! I can get by easily, just living in a couple of the rooms, but I have to hire someone to clean the whole house. Thanks, anyway.

Gary, the expensive theatre you had built in my house is beautiful. It holds 50 people, but all of my friends are dead now, so I have no one to watch movies with. And my eyes get tired so easily. But thank you for this wonderful gesture.

Larry, thank you for the lovely car. It's so big and shiny. I've never had a car so fancy. But I don't get out of the house much. I'm too old to travel. I have my groceries delivered, and when I use the Bentley to go shopping, I usually have to get someone to drive me because my eyesight isn't what it used to be. But thank you; the thought was a good one.

Harry, you were the only son to have the good sense to put some thought into your gift. The chicken was delicious. Thank you!

JEFF AND MOLLY

JEFF AND MOLLY were high school sweethearts. Some say they were made for each other. They got married soon after graduation and embarked on a lifetime of married bliss.

But things didn't go as well as they'd planned. In order to afford their modest home, both Jeff and Molly had to work, and neither had a college degree. Molly tried waitressing for awhile, but the restaurant she worked at closed, and no one else was hiring – not even the fast food places. Jeff worked in a local factory until the layoffs came last year. Since then, he tried to pick up some cash working as a mechanic and doing odd jobs.

Jeff was tremendously proud of his days as a star quarterback on the Franklin High football team. Molly was the head cheerleader at Franklin, easily identified by her trademark beautiful, long, natural-blonde hair. She was so proud of her hair that Molly brushed it religiously every night before she went to bed, counting every brushstroke. Regardless of their financial situation, she always used the finest shampoos and conditioners on her magnificent locks. As for Jeff, he still had the football he carried to score the winning touchdown in the State Championship Game, and he proudly displayed it over the fireplace.

Christmas was approaching, and Jeff and Molly wanted desperately to give each other a special, meaningful gift, despite the fact that times were so tough. And each of them came up with a special, secret plan.

Christmas morning that year was especially frigid, and to save money, they kept the house at a fairly cool temperature. So, Molly came downstairs wearing a thick robe and a scarf on her head. She held Jeff's gift in a festively wrapped box. Likewise, Jeff wore a heavy robe, and presented Molly with a small, gaily wrapped package.

Molly unwrapped her gift and immediately burst into tears. The gift was a beautiful pair of sterling silver barrettes for the magnificent, flowing, blonde hair of which she was so proud.

"Why are you crying? Are those tears of joy?" Jeff wondered.

Then, Molly removed her scarf, to reveal that her long, blonde hair had been cut to a boyish bob. Tearfully, she held out Jeff's gift.

He took it, opened it, and found a beautifully carved mahogany pedestal on which he could display the football he was so proud of on the hearth.

Molly said, "I had my hair cut and sold it to buy you this hand-carved pedestal for your prized football." But, looking up, she saw that the ball was no longer on the hearth.

Jeff sheepishly said, "I sold the football to a collector to buy you the barrettes for your hair."

"You asshole!" said Molly.

A month later, she divorced him and married a rich guy.

MEMORIES

AN ELDERLY COUPLE went to their doctor for their annual physicals, and both were pronounced physically healthy, even at their advanced ages, but the doctor told them they might want to start writing things down because their memories probably weren't what they used to be.

That night, while they were watching TV, the old man got up out of his chair and his wife asked, "Where are you going?"

"To the kitchen," he said.

"Will you get me a bowl of ice cream?" his wife asked.

"Certainly," he replied.

"Aren't you going to write it down so you can remember it?" she asked. "You know the doctor suggested we start doing that."

"No," he said, "I can remember a bowl of ice cream. The doctor was just being careful."

"Well, OK," she said, "but I'd like some strawberries on top, too. You'd better write it down, now, because I know you'll forget the strawberries."

"No," he said, "I won't forget. You want a bowl of ice cream with strawberries."

"With whipped cream," she said. "I'd also like some whipped cream on top, but I'm sure you'll forget that unless you write it down."

"Now you're just trying to make it harder for me to remember," said the husband, "but it's not going to work. I don't need to write it down. I can remember ice cream, strawberries and whipped cream."

"I don't know…" his wife said.

Irritated, the husband said, "Say no more. I can remember it. Ice cream with strawberries and whipped cream. I've got it, for goodness sake!" And he stalked out of the room.

20 minutes later, the husband finally emerged from the kitchen and handed his wife a plate of bacon and eggs.

She stared at the plate for a moment and said, "Where's my toast?"

THE MOOSE HUNTERS

B ILLY BOB AND Cletus were a couple of good ol' boys from the hills. And, of course, one of their greatest loves was hunting. The year before, they had the time of their lives when they traveled up to Western Canada, where they hunted moose. So, this year, they were anxious to return to the Canadian wilderness and, once again, show off their prowess as outdoorsmen.

And the boys managed to bag six moose.

Unfortunately, the only way to get to the hunting grounds, in the far reaches of northern Canada where herds of moose roamed, was by way of a small, single engine airplane, which Billy Bob and Cletus hired for the job. When the pilot saw the six huge moose, he informed them that they would be way over the weight limit for his aircraft. The plane could take only three moose.

Billy Bob and Cletus objected loudly and strongly. They told the pilot, "Last year, we shot six moose, and the pilot had the same kinda plane y'all have! He put ever' last one of 'em on board with nary a word."

Embarrassed, the pilot reluctantly gave in, and all six moose were loaded aboard. Unfortunately, even at full power, the little plane struggled to clear the trees on takeoff, and went down in the deep, dark wilderness a few minutes later. Miraculously, no one was killed.

Climbing out of the wreckage, Billy Bob asked Cletus, "Where do ya reckon we are? Any idea?"

Cletus replied, "I think we're pretty close to where we crashed last year."

Happy Endings

LATE ARRIVAL

O'BRIEN STAGGERED HOME very late after another evening with his drinking buddies. He took off his shoes to avoid waking his wife, Mary. Then, he tiptoed as quietly as he could toward the stairs leading to their upstairs bedroom but misjudged the bottom step. It was all he could do to catch himself by grabbing the banister, but as he did so, his body swung around, and he landed heavily on his rump.

It wasn't a good time for O'Brien to have a whiskey bottle in each back pocket. Both bottles shattered and made his landing especially painful.

O'Brien managed to stifle a scream that would have awakened not only Mary but surely the neighbors as well. He sprung up, pulled down his pants, and looked in the hall mirror to see that his rear end was cut and bleeding in several places.

He tiptoed to the kitchen and found a full box of Band-Aids, then returned to the full-length hall mirror, where he began putting Band-Aids as best he could on each place he saw blood. He then hid the almost-empty Band-Aid box, and painfully stumbled up the stairs and into bed.

The next morning, O'Brien awoke with a throbbing pain in his head, and a terrible, burning pain in his buttocks. Worse yet, Mary was staring at him from across the room, with an angry look on her face.

She said, "You were drunk again last night, weren't ya?"

O'Brien said, "Now why would ye say such a mean thing?"

"Well," Mary said, "It could be the front door that ya left open. Or it could be the broken whiskey bottle glass at the bottom of the stairs. It could be the drops of blood ya trailed through the kitchen, up the stairs and into the bed. Or it could just be yer bloodshot eyes. But mostly it's those Band-Aids stuck on the hall mirror!"

THE SENSITIVE MAN

THEY MET IN an upscale bar that catered to singles but wasn't your typical, crowded, noisy "pickup joint." She came there about once a week, but this was the first time she saw him. He was tall with sandy hair and green eyes. She was an attractive brunette. They talked. They connected. They ended up leaving together and going to his place, which was within walking distance.

He showed her around his apartment, which, she thought, was remarkably neat and clean for a single guy's living quarters. But what struck her as most unusual was his enormous collection of teddy bears. One wall of his bedroom was completely filled with dozens of soft, sweet, cuddly teddy bears of all sizes.

It was obvious that he had taken quite some time to lovingly arrange his collection of bears, and she was touched by the amount of thought he had put into organizing the display. This was surely the work of a sensitive man. The bears were arranged on three shelves that stretched along the entire wall with small bears displayed all along the bottom shelf, medium-size bears covering the length of the middle shelf, and huge stuffed bears positioned all along the top shelf.

She found it strange for such a masculine guy to have such a large collection of stuffed teddy bears, but she didn't mention this to him because she didn't want to risk offending him. And, actually, she was quite impressed by this sensitive side of him.

They shared a bottle of wine and engaged in fascinating conversation. After awhile, she thought to herself, "Maybe this guy could be the one! It certainly appears he would make a wonderful, sensitive family man.

They kissed, and the passion built. Soon, he romantically lifted her into his arms and carried her into the bedroom, where they made love. She was so overwhelmed that she responded with more passion, more creativity, and more heat than she had ever known.

After an intense, explosive night of lovemaking, as they were lying next to each other in bed enjoying the afterglow, she rolled onto her side, gently stroked his chest, and coyly said, "Well, how was it?"

He rolled onto his side, smiled at her, gently touched her cheek, looked deeply into her eyes and said, "Help yourself to any prize from the middle shelf!"

RADICAL PROCEDURE

JOE WAS MODERATELY successful in his career, but as he got older he was increasingly hampered by incredible headaches. When both his work and his personal life began to suffer, Joe sought medical help. He was referred to a specialist who diagnosed the problem and had a solution.

The doctor said, "Joe, the good news is that I can cure those terrible headaches you've been having. The horrible news is that it will require a radical procedure: castration. You have a very rare condition that causes your testicles to press up against the base of your spine, and the pressure creates the painful headaches you're been experiencing. The only way to relieve that pressure is to remove the testicles."

Joe was shocked and depressed but saw no alternative. The headaches were simply unbearable; he just couldn't live with them any longer. So, he had the operation.

When he left the hospital, Joe had mixed emotions. He was now missing an important part of himself, but he also realized that, for the first time in 20 years, he didn't have a headache. As he walked down the street, he realized that now would be the perfect time to make a new beginning and live a new and better life. And he thought, what better way to embark on an exciting, new life than with a brand-new suit, custom-fit by a tailor!

Joe stopped in a men's clothing store, and told the salesman, "I'd like a new suit."

The elderly tailor eyed him briefly and said, "Let's see…size 42 long."

Joe smiled and said, "That's right. How did you know?"

The little old tailor said, "I've been in the business over 60 years. I can tell."

Joe tried on the suit and it fit perfectly. The salesman asked,

"How about a new shirt?"

Joe said, "Why not?" And the old tailor said, "Hmmnn...17 inch neck and 34 sleeves."

Joe said, "Right again! How did you know?"

The elderly tailor said, "I've been in business more than 60 years. Over the years, you learn things – tricks of the trade, and everything there is to know about men's wear."

Of course, the shirt fit perfectly, so the salesman said, "To complete the package, how about some sox and new underwear?"

Joe said, "Everything fits so perfectly, we may as well go all the way and get a few pairs of sox and underwear, too."

They picked out some sox, and turned their attention toward underwear. The little tailor said, "Hmmnn, let's see now...you prefer briefs...I'd say a size 36 will do nicely."

Joe laughed and said, "A-ha! I've got you, this time! I've been wearing size 32 briefs since I was 18 years old!"

The old tailor shook his head and said, "You can't wear a size 32, son. A size 32 would press your testicles up against the base of your spine and give you one hell of a headache!"

ONE NIGHT AT THE FARM

AN EAST INDIAN from Calcutta, a Jew, and a lawyer were driving through the country late one night when their car broke down. Needing a place to sleep for the night and nowhere near a motel, they began walking and stopped at the first farmhouse they saw.

Each of the men offered the farmer $50 to let them sleep there for the night. The friendly farmer agreed but said, "I only have room in the house for two of you. One of you will have to sleep in the barn." The East Indian said, "That's OK, I come from humble beginnings. I'll sleep in the barn." And he walked off to sleep in the barn.

A little while later, there was a knock at the door. The farmer opened it, and the East Indian was standing there. He said, "I did not know you had a cow, and cattle are sacred in my religion. I cannot sleep in the barn with a cow."

So, the Jewish man said, "That's alright, *I'll* sleep in the barn." And off he went.

A short time later, there was a knock at the door. The farmer opened it, and the Jewish man was standing there. He said, "There is a pig in the barn. It is against my religion to sleep in the barn with a pig."

So, the lawyer says, "Fine. I guess then *I'll* sleep in the barn." And off he went.

A few minutes later, there was a knock at the door. The farmer opened it, and there, standing on the porch, were the cow and the pig.

THE ENCOUNTER

A SALESMAN WAS on yet another of what seemed like an interminable number of business trips. Another city, another hotel. Feeling lonely, he headed down to the hotel bar and, before long, an attractive, young lady walked in and sat down. He immediately decided to approach her before someone else did, start a conversation, and see where things might lead.

They moved to a table for two, and over the course of the next two hours, they learned a lot about each other. But one fact stood out among all the rest that got the salesman particularly excited: the woman said she was a nymphomaniac and had been with a lot of men.

As the evening wore on, the guy decided to make his move. He said, "I hate to talk shop, but in your experience, which guys are the best lovers?"

She thought for a moment and said, "Indians."

"East Indians?" he asked.

"No, American Indians," she replied.

"OK," he said, "which guys make the *second* best lovers?"

"Hmmnn...Jewish guys," she said. "By the way, what did you say your name was?"

"Tonto Goldberg!"

THE AMAZING ARMAND

AFTER MANY YEARS of marriage, the couple finally had the opportunity to enjoy a vacation in Paris. They decided to go off the beaten path and experience the legendary Parisian nightlife they had read about over all these years. They wanted to spend the evening at risqué night clubs like Le Moulin Rouge and nightlife like they had seen in movies like *Cabaret*.

Thus, the couple found themselves in a small, dark cabaret, where they watched the dancing girls and drank wine. Then "The Amazing Armand" was introduced. He was a 75-year-old man and surprisingly fit for his age. He took the stage dressed in a robe and carrying a table with two walnuts on it. Music began, and the old man suddenly whipped off his robe and stood naked before the audience. He grabbed his erect penis and – Bam! Bam! – he cracked open both walnuts! The crowd – many of whom had come to the club just to see The Amazing Armand – went wild! The old man simply put his robe back on, bowed, and left the stage.

Five years later, the couple returned to Paris, and decided to see if The Amazing Armand was still in business at the age of 80. They returned to the cabaret and – sure enough – The Amazing Armand was appearing there that night!

The Amazing Armand took the stage in his robe, but this time he was carrying a table with two *coconuts* on it! The music began, he whipped off his robe, grabbed his penis, and – Bam! Bam! – cracked open both coconuts! The place went absolutely wild! The 80-year-old man put his robe back on, bowed, and left the stage.

The couple was astonished and went backstage to congratulate Armand. "We thought cracking open walnuts was great, but now, five years later, this is absolutely amazing! Why did you switch to coconuts?"

"Well," said The Amazing Armand, "my eyes aren't as good as they used to be…"

BOBBY AND BILLY

Bobby and Billy were the best of friends. They were both just six years old, with Bobby being older by about four months, and they would be starting elementary school together in September.

Bobby and Billy were inseparable. They lived next door to each other, and played catch, football, and soccer on the wide expanse of lawn that separated their houses. They played other games, watched TV at each other's houses, and often had lunch together – with their mothers' permission, of course. Being best friends, Bobby and Billy often discussed personal things that only the closest of friends talked about.

So it was quite surprising when, one afternoon, the two boys were sitting in Bobby's back yard, talking quietly, and suddenly Billy began to cry. Inconsolable, he stood up and ran home. He slammed the door behind him and fled up to his room.

The two mothers approached Bobby and asked, "Bobby, what happened? What's wrong with Billy?"

Bobby replied, "I dunno…Billy was telling me that his Mom would be taking him to the hospital tomorrow, to get a circumcision before school starts in the Fall, and how his doctor told him it wouldn't hurt a bit."

The moms said, "OK…then what happened?"

Bobby continued, "All I said to Billy was, 'Are you kidding? I had one of those when I was just a couple days old, and *I* couldn't walk for a *year!*'"

BEING NEIGHBORLY

B RIAN'S WIFE KELLY was easily the most attractive woman in the neighborhood. One Saturday morning, she had just gotten out of the shower and was wrapped in a towel. Brian was just stepping into the shower when the doorbell rang, and Kelly ran downstairs to answer the door.

When she opened the door, their neighbor, Bill, was standing on the porch. Seeing her dressed only in a towel, Bill's jaw dropped and his glasses began to fog. He reached in his pocket and pulled out two hundred dollar bills, and said, "Kelly, these two hundred dollar bills are yours if you just let that towel fall to your waist!"

Figuring it wasn't that big of a deal and, after all, they were neighbors, so he'd seen her in a bikini in the back yard, Kelly said, "Heck, why not? Two hundred bucks is two hundred bucks!" She let the towel drop to her waist and grabbed the $200.

Bill gasped at the sight, and she was certain she saw a little drool in the corner of his mouth. He reached back into his pocket, removed another $200, managed to regain his voice, and said, "I'll give you another $200 if you let the towel hit the floor!"

Kelly figured, "Well, I've gone this far, so for another 200 bucks why not?" And she dropped the towel to the ground.

Bill looked for a moment, appreciatively, thanked her profusely, gave her the other two hundred dollar bills and backed off the porch, almost falling into the shrubs.

By the time Kelly got back upstairs, Brian was out of the shower. He asked Kelly who was at the door.

"Just Bill, from next door," she said.

And Brian replied, "Did he say anything about paying back the $400 he owes me?"

POLISH SAUSAGE

*I*GREW UP *in a Polish neighborhood and spent 12 years in a school that was more than three-quarters Polish. So, growing up, I must have heard hundreds of funny Polish stories. This is just one of them.*

A guy walked into a store and said to the clerk, "I would like some Polish sausage. Some Kielbasa. Do you have any Polish sausage?"

The clerk looked at him and said, "Are you Polish?"

The man was offended. He said, "As a matter of fact, yes, I am Polish. But if I had asked for Italian sausage would you ask me if I'm Italian? If I asked for yogurt, would you ask me if I'm Greek? If I wanted a taco or burrito, would you ask me if I'm Mexican?"

The clerk said, "Well...no...but..."

His anger building, the guy continued, "So, why do you ask me if I'm Polish just because I came in here and asked for Polish sausage?"

The clerk said, "Because this is a hardware store."

NO BABY TALK!

THIS WAS THE Big Time: First Grade. No more Kindergarten! Now, the former Kindergarteners were trying to become accustomed to the hurdles of First Grade. Like going to school all day. No more nap-time. And the teacher insisting on "no baby talk."

Every day, the teacher would remind them to "use *big people* words." So, when she asked Erin what she had done over the weekend, and Erin answered, "I went to visit my Nana," the teacher said, "No, Erin, you went to visit your *Grandmother*. We're using *big* people words now!"

Next, the teacher asked Joshua what he had done over the weekend. Joshua said, "I went to the zoo with my family, and we all took a ride on the choo-choo!"

"No, Joshua," said the teacher, "You took a ride on the *train*. We're using *big* people words now, so you should say *train* instead of *choo-choo!*"

Then, the teacher called on Kevin. "Kevin, what did you do this weekend?" she asked.

"I read a whole book," he replied.

"Oh, my! That's wonderful," said his teacher. "What book did you read?"

Kevin thought for a few seconds, then puffed out his chest and proudly announced, "Winnie the Shit!"

SOLITUDE

FTER A CAREER as a naval officer, Bob figured he'd had enough stress in his lifetime. He retired and bought 50 acres of land in Michigan's sparsely populated Upper Peninsula. Now he was officially a "Yooper," ready to enjoy life as far from humanity as possible.

Bob saw the postman once a week. He bought his groceries once a month, did all his own home repairs, and had to drive 20 miles to the nearest big town for anything more than bread and milk, which he was able to buy, in a pinch, at a gas station food mart. Otherwise, it was total peace and quiet; the nearest neighbor was four miles away.

After 6 months or so of almost total isolation, Bob was finishing dinner when he heard a knock at his door. He opened it, and there was a big, bearded lumberjack type standing there.

"Name's Enoch," he said, "Your neighbor from four miles down the road, other side of the lake. Havin' a party Saturday night. Thought you'd like to come."

"Sure!" said Bob. "After 6 months of quiet, I'm ready to meet some local folks. Thanks! My name's Bob!"

"OK, Bob, see ya there," said Enoch, and he gave Bob directions. But, as he was leaving, he said, "Gotta warn ya, though, there's gonna be some drinkin.'"

"No problem," said Bob, "After 25 years in the Navy, I can do that with the best of 'em."

Again, as he was about to leave, Enoch stopped. "More 'n' likely, Bob, might be some fightin' too."

Damn, Bob thought. Tough crowd. Must be from living up here by themselves. He said, "Well, Enoch, I get along pretty well with folks. I'll be there. Thanks, again."

Once again, as he was about to step off the porch, Enoch turned and said, "Y'know, there just might be some wild sex at this party, too.

I've seen it before at these parties."

"Now, that's *definitely* not a problem," Bob said, smiling. "Remember, I've been up here alone for the past 6 months! I'll be there for sure! Uh, by the way, what should I wear to the party?"

Walking away, Enoch said over his shoulder, "Whatever you want. It's just gonna be the two of us!"

BIG HELP

John Williams Tipton was a wealthy man. He lived alone, in a large mansion, in the best part of town. One Saturday afternoon, Tipton was in his reading room, deeply engrossed in a best-selling novel, when his doorbell rang. Tipton answered the door and found a disheveled young man on his doorstep. The man appeared to be homeless. His clothes were dirty; his hair unkempt. But he had a brilliant smile and an eager-to-please attitude. He was doing the best he could under the circumstances.

The man said, "Good afternoon, sir. My name is Bill Waters. I'm out of work, and I really need some money, but I don't want to take charity. I'm willing to work, and I'll do anything. Do you need your lawn mowed or your hedges trimmed?"

Tipton said, "Well, the gardener takes care of the lawn and landscaping, but look, I can see you need the work, and you're a very personable man. Can you paint?"

"Yes, sir, I sure can!" said Bill. "I can do any kind of painting you want done."

"Fine," said Tipton. "Go around back, behind the house, take some gray paint out of the tool shed, and paint my porch back there. You'll find everything you need in the shed. When you're finished, just ring the doorbell, and I'll pay you $100 for your work."

"That's very generous, sir! Thank you!" said Bill.

A few hours later, the doorbell rang, and Tipton opened the front door to find Bill standing there.

"All finished, sir," said Bill, "And I must say, it looks great! But there's just one thing I've gotta tell ya."

"What's that?" said Tipton.

"That ain't a porch you've got back there. It's a Ferrari!"

HEALTHY LIFESTYLE

Roy and Mildred were 85 years old and had been married for 60 years. Though they were far from wealthy, they managed to get by because they watched their pennies. Though they were not young, they were both in very good health because, for the past decade, Mildred insisted they eat nothing but healthy foods, and that they exercise every day.

Unfortunately, their good health didn't help them because one day, as they were headed to Florida on a rare vacation, their plane crashed, sending Roy and Mildred off to Heaven.

St. Peter showed them a beautiful mansion, expensively furnished, with a fully stocked kitchen, a complete library and reading room, an entertainment center, and closets filled with their favorite clothes. Being frugal, Roy asked, "How much will all of this cost?"

St. Peter answered, "Why, nothing! You're in Heaven now. This will be your home."

Roy looked out the window and saw a championship golf course, right outside his home. "What are the greens fees if I want to play golf?" he asked.

"This is Heaven," St. Peter replied. "You can play here for free, every day."

Next, they went to the clubhouse and saw a lavish buffet with every imaginable cuisine displayed before them, including seafood, steaks, rich sauces and gravies, fresh fruits, exotic dishes, luscious desserts, and free-flowing beverages of all kinds.

St. Peter glanced at Roy and said, "Don't even ask. This is Heaven. All of this food and drink is free for you to enjoy."

Roy glanced nervously at Mildred, and said, "But where are the low fat and low cholesterol foods? Where is the skim milk and decaffeinated coffee and tea?"

"That's the best part," said St. Peter. "You can eat and drink as much as you like of whatever you like, and you will never get fat or sick. This is Heaven!"

Roy glared at Mildred and said, "You and your damn wheat germ, bran muffins and exercise! We could have been here 10 years ago!"

PLAYING THROUGH

Rick and Kevin were dedicated golfers. One day, they were standing on the 4th tee, overlooking the river, and rain was coming down in buckets. A real cloudburst. Rick gestured down toward the river where two men were fishing and said, "Look at those two idiots down there, fishin' in the rain!"

Later, the weather cleared, so Rick and Kevin played the back nine, but after a few holes, they found they were having an awfully slow round of golf. The reason was they were following a pair of attractive women, who managed to hit every sand trap, every water hazard, and every rough. More importantly, it appeared that the women were unaware that it would be proper golf etiquette to allow Rick and Kevin to play on through.

After two hours of waiting and waiting, Rick said, "I think I'll walk up there and ask those ladies to let us play through." He walked up the fairway, got halfway to the women, stopped, turned around, and hastily returned with a sheepish look on his face.

"What's up?" Kevin asked.

"I can't do it," Rick said. "As luck would have it, one of those women is my wife and the other is my mistress! Would you, please, go talk to them?"

"Sure," said Kevin, and walked off. He got halfway to the women, stopped, turned around, and quickly walked back.

"What's up?" Rick asked.

Shaking his head sadly, Kevin said, "Small world."

BEAR FACTS

MORE AND MORE people are taking to the Great Outdoors. National Parks and wilderness areas are seeing more visitors than ever before. In addition, cities have spread far beyond their original borders, and forests are being replaced by housing. This is particularly true in once-sparsely populated areas of the country such as Montana and Wyoming.

Recently, the Wyoming Department of Fish and Game began advising hikers, campers, hunters, and fishermen to take extra precautions when they are in the wild and to remain watchful for signs of bears while they are in the field.

The advisory said:

Except during hunting season, we advise outdoorsmen to wear noisy little bells on their clothing, so as not to startle bears that aren't expecting them. We also advise outdoorsmen to carry cans of pepper spray with them, which they may use in case of an encounter with a bear.

It is also a good idea to watch out for fresh signs of recent bear activity. Black bears, while large and dangerous in the wild, are somewhat smaller and less imposing than Grizzly bears, which are larger, meaner, more volatile, and more unpredictable. So, it is important that outdoorsmen recognize the difference between black bear and grizzly bear droppings:

Black bear droppings are smaller and contain lots of berries and squirrel fur and bones.

Grizzly bear droppings are larger. They often contain little bells and smell like pepper.

THE BIG DECISION

B EN WOKE UP in the hospital, bandaged from head to foot. He had just regained consciousness when the doctor came in and said, "Ah, you're awake! Now, you probably don't remember, but you were in a terrible traffic accident on the freeway. Now, you're going to be fine. You have several broken bones, but your arms and legs will heal, and you'll walk again. There are no internal injuries. However, I don't know how to break this to you except in a straightforward manner: Your penis was amputated in the wreck, and responders were unable to find it."

Ben groaned at this horrible news, but the doctor continued, "The good news is that we now have the technology to reconstruct a penis for you, but it doesn't come cheap. The cost is $1,000 per inch. The better news is that your insurance will pay you $9,000 in compensation, regardless of what you choose, so it's just a matter of your deciding how many inches you want."

Ben perked up at this great news, and the doctor continued, "Now, we strongly recommend that you discuss this with your wife because if you ask for a penis that is larger than the one you had, she may be annoyed. However, if you decide to get one that's much smaller, she may be disappointed. It's very important that she play a role in making this decision.

So, Ben agreed to talk with his wife.

The doctor returned the next day and said, "Have you spoken with your wife?"

"I have," said Ben.

"And has she helped you arrive at a decision?"

"She has," said Ben.

"And what is it?" asked the doctor.

"We're getting a new kitchen."

Happy Endings

HOTEL BILL

A HUSBAND AND wife were driving from Florida to Boston, and after a long day on the road, they were just too tired to continue. There was no vacancy at the motels they passed, and their only alternative was a big hotel in Atlantic City. So, they decided to stop and take a room. They figured that, since they planned to sleep only five hours before getting back on the road, and wouldn't be using any of the hotel's amenities, the cost of a room wouldn't be too high.

When they checked out five hours later, the clerk gave them a bill for $350. The husband exploded; he wanted to know why the charge was so high for using a room for only five hours. He thought the hotel would give him a break, knowing how late they'd checked in and how brief their stay was. It was a nice hotel, but the room certainly wasn't worth $350 for five hours.

"$350 is our standard rate," said the clerk. So the man asked to speak to the Manager.

The Manager appeared, listened to the man, and then explained that the hotel had a casino, an Olympic-sized pool, a huge conference center, Wi-Fi, concierge, gift shops, several restaurants, and other amenities the man and his wife could have used.

"But we didn't use them. We weren't here long enough," said the husband.

"Well, they are here, and you could have," explained the Manager. He went on to further explain that the couple could have enjoyed one of the stage shows for which the hotel is famous. "The best entertainers from New York, Las Vegas and around the world perform here," he said.

"But we didn't go to any of those shows," said the man.

"Well, we have them, and you could have," the Manager replied.

No matter what facility or amenity the Manager mentioned, the man reminded him they didn't use it in the five hours they were there. But the Manager still insisted, "Well, it was here, and you could have used it."

Finally, the man wrote a check and gave it to the Manager, who looked at the check and saw it was made out for only $50.

"But sir, this check is made out for only $50, not $350," said the Manager.

"That's correct," said the husband. "I charged you $300 for sleeping with my wife."

"But I didn't sleep with your wife, sir!" exclaimed the Manager.

"Well, too bad," the man replied. "She was here and you could have!"

THE MAN AND THE MOUSE

A BEDRAGGLED, MANGY-LOOKING guy wandered into a bar and ordered a drink. The bartender immediately protested, saying, "No way, sir. I don't think you can pay for it."

"You're right, said the ragged guy. I don't have any money. But if I show you something entertaining that you've never seen before, would that be worth a drink?"

"Well, sure," said the bartender, "as long as it isn't risqué or illegal."

"Deal!" said the guy. He reached into his coat pocket and pulled out a white mouse. He gently put the mouse down on the bar, and told the bartender and patrons not to worry or be afraid of it. The mouse ran to the end of the bar, down the bar, across the room, up the piano, and onto the keyboard, where he started playing and singing Billy Joel's "Piano Man," then followed with a Gershwin tune, and an old standard recently made popular again by Rod Stewart.

The bar patrons burst into applause, and the bartender was amazed. Not only could the mouse play piano and sing, but he was really good, too!

The unkempt man drank his drink and asked for another, but the bartender said, "I'm sorry, I'll give you a second drink, but I'll have to stop there. If you want more, you'll need money or another miracle."

So, the guy reached into his threadbare coat and produced a frog. He set the frog down on the bar, and the frog started to sing. He had an excellent voice and perfect pitch.

A stranger from the other end of the bar offered the bum $300 for the frog, and the guy said, "It's a deal!" He took the money, and the stranger grabbed the frog and ran out of the bar.

"Are you nuts?" shouted the bartender. "You sold a singing frog for $300? It must have been worth millions! You could have cleaned up, bought new clothes, and become famous! You must be crazy!"

"I'm not crazy," said the mangy-looking guy. "That frog is worthless. The mouse is also a ventriloquist!"

AN OLD WESTERN TALE

THE OLD WEST is filled with amazing tales and rituals, many of which live on to this very day.

A hunter was hunting in a mountainous, isolated part of the Old West with two Indian guides. As they were walking through the deep woods, they came upon a cave. One of the Indian guides ran up to the cave, stood at the mouth of the cave, and shouted "Wooo wooo!" He did this repeatedly until, from within the darkness of the cave, he heard a reply very similar to the sound he made: "Wooo wooo!" Upon hearing this, the Indian guide tore off his clothes and raced into the cave.

The hunter was puzzled, until the other Indian guide explained, "Him find-um beautiful squaw who live in cave. Him stay with her and not come out today. We go."

So, the hunt continued. They passed other caves, but the second Indian guide ignored them. Then, they spotted a cave similar to the first. The Indian guide raced to the mouth of the cave and shouted in a high-pitched voice, "Wooo wooo!" He did this several times, until from within the cave he heard, "Wooo wooo!" The Indian guide then shed his clothes, raced into the cave, and didn't come out.

Now, the guy was hunting alone, in unfamiliar territory. He envied the Indian guides' good fortune in finding squaws in this most unusual way because he, himself, hadn't been with a woman for several months. Just then, he came upon a cave that he thought looked just like the two large caves into which the Indian guides had disappeared. He approached the mouth of the cave, and imitating the sound the two Indians made, he shouted, "Wooo wooo!" He repeated this several times, and – wonder of wonders – he heard a response: "Wooo wooo!" The hunter tore off his clothes, and raced into the cave.

The next day, the headline in the local newspaper read: HUNTER KILLED BY TRAIN!

ANOTHER OLD WESTERN TALE

ONE DAY IN the Old West, a stagecoach was about to leave town for its destination, 60 miles west, straight through Indian country. The journey was a treacherous one, made worse by the fact that the driver had no one to ride shotgun next to him. His regular shotgun guard, whose job was to protect the precious Wells Fargo box and fight off robbers and Indians, was ill that day. But the run had to be made as scheduled, and soon a little, old guy volunteered to ride shotgun even though he had never ridden shotgun in his life – or even handled a shotgun! In fact, his vision wasn't too great, either!

But the stagecoach had to leave, and leave it did. Soon, they were in Indian territory, and the driver nudged the old man and said, "Look! Out there in the distance! That tiny figure! Is that an Indian?"

The old guy squinted at the tiny figure and said, "I dunno! He's just a little, tiny figure!"

They rode farther, and the figure became larger. It appeared to be a man on a horse. An Indian? "I still can't tell!" said the little old shotgun guard, holding his fingers an inch apart. "He's only this big!"

Later, the figure came closer, and they could now make out feathers. An Indian! But it looked like he was alone, so they pressed onward.

Still later, they saw that the Indian was wearing war paint, and he turned towards them and began charging the stagecoach. Soon, he was joined by other Indians, charging behind him!

The driver pointed at the lead Indian and shouted, "Shoot him, you fool! Shoot him!"

The old shotgun guard said, "I can't!"

"Why not?" said the driver.

The old man held his fingers an inch apart and said, "I've known him since he was *this big!*"

SATURDAY AT THE BARBERSHOP

RAY WAS A barber. After 10 years of running his barbershop in the downtown area of a thriving suburb, he had a pretty regular clientele. In fact, Saturdays, when most guys stopped in for a haircut because they worked during the week, were so busy that Ray was contemplating adding a second chair and barber. But Ray's clients loved his work, and they didn't mind waiting for an hour or more, if necessary, reading, watching TV, and talking about sports and local politics with friends.

But, every Saturday afternoon, for several weeks, a young guy whom Ray didn't recognize would open the door, stick his head in, and ask, "How long do I have to wait before I can get a haircut?" Each time, Ray would look around, see all the customers waiting, and say, "About an hour." The guy would thank Ray and leave, but he never returned for a haircut.

After a full month of having the guy poke his head in during the busiest time every Saturday, ask how long the wait was, then leave, Ray looked over at a teenaged boy who was waiting for a haircut, and said, "Hey, Dean! Why don't you follow that guy who just stuck his head in here, and see where he goes? He always shows up at my busiest time, asks about the waiting time, and never comes back for a haircut. Maybe he's going to a salon down the street. I'd like to know what he's up to."

About 30 minutes later, Dean returned to the barbershop, grinning from ear to ear.

"Well," said Ray, "Did you see where he went?"

Dean replied, "Yeah! To *your* house!"

THE LUCKY IRISH GOLFER

ONE FINE DAY in Ireland, a man was out golfing. At the 13th hole, he teed up and took a mighty swing but sliced his drive deep into the woods that ran along the right side of the fairway.

While looking for his golf ball, the man came across a little guy lying flat on the ground with a huge knot on his forehead and the golf ball lying on the grass right beside him. "Goodness," said the golfer, who proceeded to revive the poor little guy.

Upon awakening, the little man said, "Well, sure an' ya caught me fair an' square, ya did! I am a leprechaun, and I will grant ye three wishes."

The golfer says, "Oh, no. I can't take anything from you. I'm just glad I didn't hurt you too badly. If you're sure you're OK, I'll just be on my way." And he walked away and continued playing the hole.

The leprechaun was amazed that anyone could turn down three wishes, but he had his tradition to live up to, and said, "Well he was a nice enough lad, and he *did* catch me, so I'm obligated to do something for him. I'll just give him three things that *I* would want! I'll give him unlimited money…fantastic golfing abilities…and, to top it off…a great sex life!"

A year went by, and the same golfer came to the 13th hole on the same golf course. He told his friends to play through and walked into the woods where he met the leprechaun a year before. He found him, and asked how he was doing.

"Sure and I'm fit as a fiddle," said the leprechaun. "But how have *ye* been? Pretty good, I'll wager," he said, smiling happily.

"My golf game is outstanding," said the golfer. "I'm a scratch golfer, usually at or under par every time I play."

"And how is your money holding out?" the leprechaun asked with a knowing grin.

"Now that you mention it, since we met, every time I put my hand in my pocket this past year, I've found just enough money to pay whatever expense I've had!" said the golfer.

The leprechaun smiled and proudly said, "Sure an' I did that for ya! You caught me fair an' square that day a year ago! And," he said slyly, "might I be askin' how yer sex life is?"

Now, the golfer was embarrassed. He looked at the leprechaun sheepishly, and mumbled, "Well...um...maybe once or twice a week..."

The leprechaun was floored! He stammered, "Only once or twice a week!?"

The golfer sat up straight, mustered up his dignity, and said, "Well, that's not bad for a priest in a small parish!"

CHEAP MOTEL

A HUSBAND AND wife were traveling. It was late at night, and they hadn't made reservations at any motel along the way, because they had no idea how far they would get when their drive began that morning. As a result, they found themselves checking into a cheap motel, next to a railroad track, just outside of a small town.

"Will that railroad track be any problem?" they asked the clerk.

"Oh, no. We rarely get any complaints about noisy trains from any of our guests," said the clerk. "In fact, trains hardly ever pass by our place anymore."

The couple agreed to take a room. They were hungry and – just their luck – the nearest restaurant was in town, a mile down the road. So, the husband went for food, and the wife was so tired from a day on the road, she just couldn't wait for him to return with it. She changed her clothes and climbed into bed.

She had just dozed off when a train rumbled past the motel, and the vibration was so tremendous that it knocked her right out of bed!

Figuring this was just a weird, unusual occurrence, she climbed back into bed and dozed off. Moments later, another train rumbled by with such force it knocked her out of bed. This time, she called the front desk and complained.

"Ma'am, I find that hard to believe," said the clerk. "No one has ever complained about trains going by and, frankly, I think it would be impossible for it to knock you right out of bed!"

"Well, come over here and see for yourself!" she shouted, angrily.

A short time later, the husband returned with the food, and found his wife in bed with the desk clerk.

"Hey! Whaddaya think you're doing!?" he shouted.

The clerk said, "Waiting for a train?"

HIS DYING WISH

A LOT OF people loved old George. So, when he went to the hospital, he had a lot of visitors. Friends, relatives, co-workers, even the pastor of his church came to say hello to George, wish him well, and chat awhile.

George wasn't in the greatest shape just then. He was hooked up to various machines while lying in his hospital bed, but he was expected to pull through. But then, one evening when his bed was completely surrounded by well-wishers, he unexpectedly took a turn for the worse.

George suddenly looked at the minister from his church, who was the closest to him, and frantically began gesturing for a pen and a piece of paper – something to write on. The kindly old pastor reached into his jacket pocket, removed a beautiful gold pen, and lovingly handed the pen to George, along with a piece of notepaper. And George, with his last ounce of strength, scribbled a final note, and handed it back to the cleric.

There was a flurry of activity, as nurses and doctors converged on George's bed, but it was no use: he'd passed away. Friends and family surrounding George were understandably upset at his sudden passing, and the pastor thought it best not to look at George's final words just then. He placed the note in the pocket of his jacket and walked out.

At George's funeral, the minister was just finishing George's eulogy when he realized he was wearing the same jacket that he wore the night that George passed away, and that George's final words were on a piece of paper in his pocket. He had totally forgotten until now.

On an impulse, the pastor said, "Brothers and sisters, George handed me a note just before he died. I haven't looked at it until now, but knowing George, I'm sure there will be words of inspiration in it for us all. Here is what he said."

Opening the note, the pastor cleared his throat and read aloud: "Help! You're standing on my oxygen tube!"

WORKING HOMICIDE

DOMBROWSKI DECIDED HE wanted to be a cop. And not just a cop, but a detective. And not just a detective, but a Homicide Detective!

So, he scheduled an interview with the chief of his local police force and was so anxious and excited that he arrived at the station a full hour before his appointment.

Dombrowski had no formal training in police work, criminology, or even social work. He had never worked as a guard, a bouncer, or any type of security agent. But he really wanted to be a detective. Noting his complete lack of skill and training, but his tremendous enthusiasm, the police chief decided to give him a "test" that he made up on the spot.

"I'm going to ask you three questions," said the chief. "Number one: name two days of the week that start with 'T'."

Dombrowski immediately answered, "Today and tomorrow!"

Taken aback somewhat, the chief said, "Name two directions."

Dombrowski thought for a second and answered, "This way and that way!"

Again, the chief marveled that Dombrowski didn't give him the answers he was looking for, but his answers couldn't be considered wrong. "O.K.," the chief said, "Who shot Abraham Lincoln?"

This one stumped Dombrowski. He said, "I don't think I know the answer to that one."

The chief said, "OK, then, you go home and think about it, and we'll give you a call."

Dombrowski went home and his brother asked him, "How did it go?"

Dombrowski answered, "Great! I already got the job!"

His brother asked, "How do you know?"

Dombrowski answered, "The chief already has me working on a case!"

HOW SOW-EET IT IS!

A FARMER WANTED to start a hog farm, but all he had was three female sows. Somewhat short on cash, the farmer decided that rather than buy more pigs, he would have his pigs mated at a stud farm. So, he loaded his three sows into his pickup truck and drove them over to a farm in the next county, where they spent the afternoon mating with the boars.

Just before he left the farm, he asked the stud farmer, "How can you tell if it worked – if the sows are pregnant?"

The stud farmer said, "Well, tomorrow morning, if your sows are wallowing in the mud, that means they're pregnant. If they're grazing in the grass, they're not."

The next morning, the farmer said to his wife, "Marge, look out the window and tell me what the pigs are doing."

Marge looked out and said, "They're grazing in the grass, Zeke."

The farmer said, "Damn!" He loaded his pigs back into his pickup and drove them over to the stud farm in the next county, to try again. There, the sows spent another afternoon romping with the male pigs.

The next morning, Zeke asked his wife, "Well, Marge, what are the pigs doing today?"

And Marge said, "Sorry, Zeke. They're grazing in the grass again."

Now, Zeke was beginning to get pretty upset about the whole thing, but he loaded the sows into his truck a third time and hauled them back to the stud farm , where they again spent the afternoon mating with the boars.

The next morning, Zeke said to his wife, "Well, Marge, are the pigs wallowing in the mud or grazing in the grass this morning?"

"Actually, neither!" said Marge. "Two of them are sitting out in the back of your pickup, and the third one's in the front seat, blowing the horn!"

GAS AND SEX

ART AND SAM were driving home from work together when Art noticed he was almost out of gas.

Sam said, "You're in luck, Art! There's this gas station I heard about, just up the road here, that's running some sort of promotion. You can get free sex with a fill-up!"

Now, Art and Sam were perpetually horny, so this promotion had a lot of appeal. But Art said, "That's impossible, and it's probably illegal. How could they do that?"

But, just then, they saw the gas station, with a big sign out front that said: Ask About Our *Free Sex With Fill-Up* Deal! Naturally, they couldn't wait to try it.

As his tank was being filled, Art walked up to a tall, handsome, muscular attendant, and said, "How does this free sex with fill-up thing work? Where are the girls? In back?"

And the attendant said, "Simple, sir! Just guess the number I'm thinking of between 1 and 10, and you get free sex!"

So, Art said, "OK, six!"

And the attendant said, "Oh, I'm sorry, sir. The number I was thinking of was 9."

Then Sam said, "Is it OK if I try it?"

The attendant said, "Well, sir, it's usually open only to the driver paying for the gas, but for you, I'll make an exception. Go ahead and guess."

And Sam said, "Nine!"

"Oh, I'm sorry, sir!" said the handsome attendant. "The last number was nine, but this time the winning number was 7."

As they were pulling out of the station, Art was fuming. "What a rip-off!" he said. "Free sex my eye! That was nothing but a scam!"

And Sam said, "No, Art, it's NOT a scam! Why, just last week, my *wife* came in here *twice* and won BOTH TIMES!"

CONFESSION

FATHER O'BRIEN AND Rabbi Hurwitz were lifelong friends. They grew up together, and now Father O'Brien's parish was only a few blocks from Rabbi Hurwitz's synagogue.

The old friends enjoyed playing golf together, but when Rabbi Hurwitz showed up at Father O'Brien's church, there was still a long line for confession. So, the Rabbi walked up to the confessional, tapped on the door, and asked Father O'Brien how long it would be.

Father O'Brien said, "About 45 minutes, but, here...why don't you join me in the confessional, and you can get a good idea of what the Catholic Church is all about." So, Rabbi Hurwitz joined Father O'Brien in the confessional.

The next confessor was a woman who said she was unfaithful to her husband. Father O'Brien said, "How many times?"

She replied, "Three times, father, each time with the same man." Father O'Brien advised her not to see the man anymore and, as her penance, he told her, "Say five Our Fathers and five Hail Marys and put $10 in the poor box."

Next, a man entered the confessional, and said he'd been unfaithful to his wife. "How many times?" asked Father O'Brien.

"Three times, with a different woman each time," said the confessor. "Well," said Father O'Brien, "be faithful to your wife, say five Our Fathers and five Hail Marys, and put $10 in the poor box."

The priest turned to the rabbi and said, "See? That's how it's done. It's highly irregular, but you're a man of the cloth, so I don't think the Lord would find any harm in it. Would you like to hear the next confession?"

"Certainly! I'd be honored!" said Rabbi Hurwitz.

The next confessor was yet another woman who had been unfaithful to her husband.

"How many times?" asked Rabbi Hurwitz, taking a cue from what Father O'Brien asked the previous two parishioners.

"Oh, my! Just once!" said the woman.

"Well, then," said Rabbi Hurwitz, "For your penance, say five Our Fathers and five Hail Marys then go out and be unfaithful two more times because this week we're having a special 3-for-$10 deal!"

KILLER LUNCH

THE SCENE: A construction site where a 50-story skyscraper was being built. Martino, Rodriguez, and Makowski were close friends, who worked together and always ate their lunch together.

One day, they were sitting on a steel girder, 30 stories above the ground, ready to have lunch. Martino opened his lunch box and took out a huge sandwich. "Salami again! I'm sick of salami! If my wife packs salami in my lunch again, I'm jumpin' off this beam!"

Then, Rodriguez opened his lunch box, and said, "Another burrito! I'm so tired of burritos I can't stand it! If I find another burrito in my lunch tomorrow, I'm gonna go right with you, Mario, and jump off this beam!"

Next, Makowski opened his lunch box and pulled out a big ham sandwich. "Crap!" he said. "Another ham sandwich! Every day, it's ham, ham, ham! If I get another ham sandwich in my lunch tomorrow, I'm gonna jump too!"

The next day, they were again sitting on the girder, 30 floors up, ready for lunch. Martino looked in his lunch box, saw a salami sandwich, and shouted, "Another salami sandwich! That does it! I can't stand it anymore!" And, true to his word, he jumped off the beam and smashed into the ground, 30 stories below.

Rodriguez pulled a burrito out of his lunch box and went ballistic. "Aiyy, another burrito! I can't stand burritos anymore! I'm jumping!" And he, too, jumped off the beam.

Then Makowski opened his lunch box, peered inside, and saw that, again, he had a ham sandwich. He screamed, "Ham again! I'm sick and tired of ham! I'm going too!" And Makowski jumped off the beam and fell 30 stories to the ground.

Two days later, the three friends were laid out together at the same funeral home. Their grieving wives were gathered together, talking about their husbands' last days.

Martino's wife said, "I can't understand why Mario would jump to his death because of a lousy salami sandwich. He always said he liked salami sandwiches the best! I guess I wasn't really listening to him when he complained about getting salami every day."

Rodriguez's wife said, "My Miguel, too. He always loved a good burrito more than anything else for lunch. Why did he do it? Why did he jump? It's all my fault!"

Finally, Makowski's wife said, "I can't understand why Joe jumped, either. He always made his own lunch!"

A MAN AND HIS CAT

RICHARD HAD A cat that followed him everywhere he went. When Richard watched TV, the cat was on his lap. When Richard ate dinner, the cat was at his feet. Even in bed, the cat often slept between Richard and his wife, Cathy.

Finally, one day, Cathy couldn't take it any longer. She said, "Richard, I'm sick of that cat! Wherever you go, the cat's there! Every time I turn around, the cat's there! Even in bed, the cat's between us! I can't take it any longer! Either the cat goes or I go!"

Richard momentarily considered the alternatives but quickly came to his senses. He realized that his marriage was more important than his love for the cat. So, with tears in his eyes, Richard drove the cat out to the country, gave him one last pet, and released him into a farmer's field, figuring that maybe the cat would be adopted by a farm family, and have a good life in the country.

When Richard got home, he shouted to Cathy, who was upstairs: "Well, I hope you're satisfied. The cat's gone. You'll never see him again. I'm gonna go make myself a drink!"

But, while Richard was making his drink, he heard a scratching at the door. He opened it, and – there was the cat!

Just then, Cathy came downstairs, saw the cat, and shouted, "What's that cat still doing here? I told you, either the cat goes or I go! What'll it be?"

Richard gave his options a little more thought this time but came to his senses and decided to get rid of the cat.

The next day, Richard drove all the way to the next town. There, he bought a bus ticket and took the cat to another rural town, where he gave the cat a hug and left it in a farmer's field.

Richard jumped back on another bus for the return trip, got back into his car, and drove home. "The cat's gone for sure, now!" he shouted to his wife, who was ironing in another room. "He'll probably get run over by a car, or attacked by some wild animal. I hope that'll make you happy!" And he settled down to watch a ballgame on TV.

Three hours later, Richard heard scratching at the door, opened it, and there was the cat again! And, once again, Cathy's timing was perfect, as she walked into the room, saw the cat, and shouted, "I thought you said you got rid of that cat! Obviously, you didn't! This is it! He goes or I go!"

Richard was speechless but determined. The next day, he drove to another town, took a different bus to a different city, and caught a train to another state. For good measure, he decided to hop a plane to yet another state, rent a car, and drive from the airport into the country with the cat riding shotgun.

Five days later, there was no sign of Richard or the cat. Cathy was talking to her mother on the phone, "They've been gone for five days now. I have no idea where they went!"

Suddenly, there was a knock at the door. Cathy opened it – and there, on the porch, were Richard and the cat!

"That cat!" she screams. "I thought I told you to get rid of it! Now, you've been gone for five days, I had no idea where you were, or if you were dead or alive, and you *still* haven't gotten rid of that damned cat!"

"Get rid of it, hell," said Richard. "If it weren't for that cat, I'd *still* be lost!"

BAD DOG!

THREE DOGS WERE in the dog pound. Like three guys in a holding tank, the dogs were asking each other what they're in for.

The first dog, a schnauzer, said, "My master got a nice, new easy chair. I kind of liked the old chair better, so I chewed up the new one while he was at the office. Next thing I know, he put me in here, and now they're gonna put me to sleep!"

The second dog, a mutt, said, "My master was going to have a barbecue in his back yard with a bunch of friends and relatives. He had just taken all of the hamburgers, hot dogs, and bratwursts off the grill, and he went inside to where his guests were watching the ballgame on the wide screen, to tell 'em the food was ready. I saw that as my opportunity for a fast lunch. I jumped up on the table and pretty much scarfed down all the burgers and brats. I was halfway through the hot dogs when he came out and went absolutely insane! Now I'm in here, and I'm gonna die in the morning!"

The third dog, a golden retriever, said, "I was innocently sitting in my master's bedroom in front of the door to the bathroom. My master's wife was undressed and leaning over the bathtub, testing the temperature of the water. I tell ya, boys, I just couldn't resist. I ran up behind her and jumped on, and ooo-weee!"

The other two dogs said, "So, you're gonna be put to death in the morning, eh? Tough luck!"

And the retriever said, "No, I'm just here to have my nails trimmed."

BENEVOLENT BARBER

STEVE RAN A small, successful barbershop on Main Street in an upscale suburb. For years, parents had been bringing their sons to Steve for their boys' first haircuts. Because Steve was adept at all the latest styles, he cut the hair of teenage boys who wouldn't be caught dead in a "girly" salon. And men came to Steve from miles around because he did good work for a fair price.

One day, Steve gave a local priest a haircut. When the priest went to pay for it, Steve said, "Oh, no thanks, Father. Just continue doing the good things you do, and that'll be payment enough for me!" The priest thanked him and left. And the next morning when Steve arrived at the barbershop, what do you suppose he found on his doorstep?

A lovely basket of assorted, fresh fruit, with a "thank you" note from the priest!

Later that week, Steve styled the hair of a local minister. When the minister went to pay for his haircut, Steve said, "Oh, no thanks, Reverend. Just keep doing the things you do, and that'll be payment enough for me!" The minister thanked him and left. The next morning, what do you suppose Steve found on his doorstep?

A huge basket, with a bottle of wine and an assortment of fine jams, jellies, and crackers!

A week later, Steve cut the hair of a local rabbi. When the rabbi went to pay for it, Steve said, "Oh, no thanks, Rabbi! Just keep on doing the good things you do, and that'll be payment enough for me!" The rabbi thanked him and left. And the next morning, when Steve arrived at the barbershop, what do you suppose he found on his doorstep?

Three more Rabbis.

GOLF – WITH AN ATTITUDE

MIKE, DAN, AND Kyle were playing golf. While they were old friends, they didn't play golf together too often. Dan was a fairly good weekend golfer while Kyle was almost a scratch golfer. He used the finest equipment and the best balls. Mike, on the other hand, had a bad hook and a terrible temper. He was not made for golf.

The threesome came to a hole with a water hazard, and Kyle and Dan drove their balls safely over the hazard onto the fairway. Mike took out a ratty old driver and a driving range ball, certain that he'd plunk one in the drink. Sure enough, he hooked his ball into the water.

Mike asked Dan if he could borrow a ball for a second try. Dan reluctantly gave him a brand new ball, and Mike promptly slammed it into the water. He then proceeded to get so mad that he took his ratty driver, swung it around his head, and threw it into the middle of the lake, about where Dan's ball had landed.

Mike then asked Kyle if he could borrow a ball and a driver from him. Kyle knew he would regret it, but he reluctantly loaned Mike his expensive driver and gave him a brand-new golf ball.

Mike teed up the ball, addressed it, took a mighty swing, and hooked the ball into the water, right where the first two had landed. He went ballistic, screaming and waving Kyle's driver. He pounded the driver into the ground, swung it over his head, and flung it as far as he could into the lake.

Kyle said, "Jeez, Mike! Take it easy! That was a brand-new $12 ball and a driver that cost me a couple hundred dollars!"

And Mike said, "Well, if you can't afford the game, don't play it!"

Happy Endings

BOBBY AND JOLENE

Bobby and Luther were talking one afternoon, and Bobby said, "Y'know, Luther, I reckon I'm 'bout ready for another vacation. Only, this year, I'm gonna do it a little different. The last few years, I took your advice about where to go for vacation, and none o' those vacations worked out quite the way I expected."

"Whut do you mean?" said Luther.

"Well, Luther," said Bobby, "three years ago, you told me to go to Hawaii. So, I went to Hawaii, and the next thing you know, the li'l missus, Jolene, is pregnant."

"So, what's wrong with that?" said Luther. "Ya got yerself a mighty find young-un."

"And, two years ago," continued Bobby, "you told me to go to the Bahamas. And dang if Jolene didn't get pregnant *again!*"

"Then, last year," Bobby said, "you suggested Tahiti for a vacation. I gotta say it's a long trip and a mighty purty place but, son of a gun if Jolene didn't get pregnant *again!*"

"So," Luther asked, "whutchu gonna do different this year, Bobby?"

Bobby thought for a few minutes, and said, "This year, Luther, I'm a-gonna take Jolene *with* me!"

MY VISIT WITH GRAMPS

IT HAD BEEN years since I spent time with Gramps. I'd been busy with work in the city, and Gramps had moved to a secluded, rural area up north. But Gramps had just turned 90, and while he seemed to be in good health, who knew how much longer he'd be around? So, I decided to pay him a visit.

Gramps lived in a cabin in the north woods. Although he had electricity, his water supply consisted of cold well water brought up from a deep well by a hand pump on his sink. And, whenever hot water was needed, he'd simply heat it in a kettle on his stove.

I arrived late, and after a couple of hours of walking down memory lane with Gramps, I went straight to bed. The next morning, I was awakened by the pleasant smell of bacon frying and coffee brewing as Gramps prepared a wonderful breakfast of bacon, eggs and toast.

As I ate, I noticed an odd film on my plate, and I laughingly asked, "Hey, Gramps, are these plates clean?"

Gramps seemed offended by my lighthearted observation, and said, "Those plates are as clean as cold water can get 'em! Now, go on and finish your meal!"

That afternoon, for lunch, we were enjoying hamburgers that Gramps made on an old barbecue out back. Again, I noticed tiny specks around the edge of my plate, and again saw that strange film on it. I said, "Gramps, are you sure these plates are clean?"

Now, Gramps was offended and annoyed. Without looking up from his food, he said, "I told you before, son, these damn plates are as clean as cold water can get 'em! Now don't ask me about 'em anymore!"

I thought that, perhaps, washing the plates in hot water might be a solution, but my grandfather's angry response encouraged me to keep my mouth shut. I didn't want to spoil my visit with my elderly grandpa.

That afternoon, I decided to treat Gramps to a nice dinner that I'd bring back from a family restaurant in town that advertised "Home Cooking." I'd spotted it the day before, on my way in. As I headed toward the door to leave, Gramps's old hound dog was laying on a rug, directly in front of the door. Not totally familiar with anyone but Gramps, the dog began to growl and wouldn't let me pass. So, I said, "Gramps, your dog won't let me out."

From across the room, where he was busy organizing his tackle box, Gramps shouted at the dog, "Dang it, Coldwater! Get out of the way!"

DON AND MARGE

Don and Marge were an elderly couple who loved to take road trips. Don loved to drive, and throughout their married life together, rarely did a summer go by without a vacation by car.

While on such a road trip, Don and Marge stopped for dinner at a nice roadside restaurant with rocking chairs on the porch. He enjoyed the Salisbury steak while she had chicken.

Soon, they were on the road again and, after about 20 minutes, Marge decided to consult the road map. It was then that she discovered she'd left her reading glasses on the table at the restaurant, where she'd needed them to read the menu. They were good, prescription glasses – not the cheap, drugstore kind – and she told Don that they'd have to turn around, return to the restaurant, and get them back.

Don's grumpy side immediately surfaced. "I don't know why you can't remember a simple thing like reading glasses. You just use them for reading – nothing else – so when you're finished with them, all you have to do is put them back in your purse." And blah blah blah.

To add to the aggravation, they had to drive another 15 miles before they had an opportunity to turn around and head back toward the restaurant, and all the way Don fussed, complained, and scolded Marge for her forgetfulness. He just wouldn't let up.

Marge quietly let him vent; there was nothing she could say or do. She'd simply forgotten her glasses.

Finally, much to Marge's relief, they arrived at the restaurant. Marge couldn't wait to get out of the car, rush inside, retrieve her glasses, and shut up the old man, who was still ranting.

After Marge got out of the car, Don rolled down the window and shouted:

"One more thing, Marge. While you're in there, you might as well get my hat and credit card, too!"

UNEMPLOYMENT ISN'T WORKING

UNEMPLOYMENT HAS BECOME a worldwide problem. Even in Ireland, which appeared to be recession-proof for a long time, jobs are hard to come by.

Recently, an engineering position opened up at an Irish firm based in Dublin. When Murphy applied for the job, he was surprised and annoyed to see that an American was there to apply for the same job. Because both men had the same qualifications, college degrees and experience, the Manager of the firm decided that the only fair approach was to have both Murphy the Irishman and Brady the American take identical written tests for the position.

Murphy and Brady were seated in a room, and both went to work answering a 10-question exam. Soon, both men completed the test, and handed them to the Manager, who took them into his office to grade them.

A short time later, the Manager emerged, and announced that both candidates had gotten 9 out of 10 questions right. Then, he walked up to Murphy, and said, "Thank you for your interest, Mr. Murphy, but I've decided to give Mr. Brady the job."

Murphy was angry. He said, "And why would you be doin' that? We both got nine questions correct, and this bein' Ireland and me bein' Irish, I should think that you'd be givin' *me* the job!"

The Manager said, "I understand, Mr. Murphy, but we based our decision not on the questions you both answered correctly, but on the one question you both missed."

"And what would that be, I'd like to know," said Murphy.

"Simple," said the Manager. "On question number seven, Mr. Brady, the American, answered, 'I don't know.'

"You wrote, 'Neither do I!'"

Happy Endings

AT THE PEARLY GATES

A CHURCH PASTOR died and was waiting in line at the Pearly Gates as St. Peter checked-in the latest group of people destined for Heaven.

Just ahead of him was a guy with slicked-down hair, dressed in jeans and a ratty leather jacket, and wearing sunglasses. St. Peter addressed him: "Who art thou, that I might admit you into the Kingdom of Heaven?"

The guy replied in a loud, boisterous voice, "Yo, Saint Pete! I am Joe Simmons, ace taxi driver, from Noo Yawk City – da greatest city inna world!"

St. Peter consulted his list, smiled, gave the taxi driver a golden staff and silken robe, and said, "Welcome, my son! Take these and enter the Kingdom of Heaven!"

The taxi driver strode into Heaven, and it was now the minister's turn.

St. Peter said, "Who art thou, that I might admit you into the Kingdom of Heaven?"

And the minister said, "St. Peter, I am David Snow, Pastor of the Community Church for the past 47 years!"

St. Peter checked his list, smiled, and gave the minister a wooden staff and cotton robe. He then said, "Welcome, Pastor, into the Kingdom of Heaven!"

The Pastor looked down at the wooden staff and cotton robe he'd been given and frowned. "Wait a minute," he said to St. Peter. "The guy in front of me was a taxi driver – and a loud, boisterous one, I might add – while I led the congregation of my church, preached the word of God, and did good deeds for well over half my life! Why did he get a golden staff and silken robe while I got a wooden staff and cotton robe? How can this be?"

St. Peter answered, "Up here, we go by the results of your actions on earth. When you preached, people slept; when he drove his cab, people prayed!"

GROOVY DATE

A<small>H, THE EARLY</small> '60s! For those of you who remember, these were innocent times – compared with today, or even compared with the late '60s. Dating was quite different then. But, as Dylan sang, "Times were a-changin'," and by the end of the decade, Woodstock, Hippies, the Swingin' Sixties, and Free Love would change everything.

It was the spring of 1962, and Danny arrived at Debbie's house to pick her up for a date. He was a pretty hip guy and quite popular in school. He was a bit more mature than many guys, with a job at the movie theater and his own car: a red Ford convertible! Danny was handsome, too, and quite a catch, as was the attractive, blue-eyed blonde, Debbie.

When Danny arrived, Debbie's father answered the door and invited Danny in. "Debbie's not ready yet," said Mr. Clark, "so why don't you have a seat, Danny?"

Debbie's Dad tried to keep up on all the latest trends. He desperately wanted Debbie's friends to like him, so she would be more popular. He wanted them to think he was like the "cool" dads they saw on TV back then. So, Debbie's Dad made an effort to be more lenient than most parents. He tried to be up-to-date, and did his best to learn the language that the kids used and know their interests. Mr. Clark asked Danny what they were planning to do that night.

Danny politely replied, "Oh, we'll just go to a movie or the soda shop, Mr. Clark."

Nodding his head and smiling, Mr. Clark said, "Hey, Danny, why don't you two go out and screw? I hear all the kids are doing it."

Naturally, these words came as quite a shock to Danny. Mr. Clark was quite the modern, forward thinker! Just to make sure, he asked Mr. Clark to repeat what he'd said.

"Oh, yeah," Debbie's Dad said, "Debbie tells me she really likes to screw. She'd screw all night if we let her!"

Well, Danny's eyes just lit up! His plans for the evening were beginning to look pretty good.

A few minutes later, Debbie came down the stairs in her little poodle skirt and told Danny and her Dad that she was ready to go.

Almost breathless with anticipation, Danny raced to the front door, opened it, said goodbye to Mr. Clark, and escorted Debbie to his car.

Less than an hour later, Mr. Clark heard the front door open. Debbie rushed back into the house, slammed the door behind her, and screamed: "Dammit, Daddy! It's called *The Twist!*"

FEELING FINE

WHILE DRIVING HIS old truck, pulling a trailer with his mule inside, Ol' Pete Jones, a farmer, had a terrible accident with a semi-truck that had run through a stop sign. A few weeks later, Pete decided to sue the trucking company that owned the truck that hit him, and eventually, he had to testify in court. Of course, the huge trucking company employed an expensive team of city lawyers, and one of them was questioning Ol' Pete.

"At the scene of the accident, Mr. Jones, didn't you say you were fine?" asked the lawyer.

"Well, I'll tell y'all what happened," said Pete. "I had just loaded my favorite mule, Bessie, into the…"

"I didn't ask for details," interrupted the lawyer. "Just answer the question, Mr. Jones. Did you not say, at the scene of the accident, that you were 'just fine'?"

"Well, I got Bessie loaded into the…" Pete began.

"Just answer the question, Mr. Jones," the lawyer interrupted again. He didn't want homespun folksiness to sidetrack his case or plant any false notions in the jury's mind. The fact was that Pete Jones told the responding police officer that he was "fine."

"OK," said Pete, "so Bessie and I were headed down the road…"

"Your honor," the lawyer interrupted again, "I am trying to establish the fact that, at the scene of the accident, this man told the Highway Patrol Officer that he was 'just fine.' Now, several weeks after the accident, he is suing my client's company, claiming to be injured. We believe he's a fraud, your honor. Please instruct him to answer my question."

But, by now, the judge was interested in what transpired leading up to the crash. He overruled the lawyer and told Pete to answer the question in his own words.

"OK," said Pete. "Like I was saying, I'd just loaded Bessie, my favorite mule, into my trailer, and was drivin' down the highway when this huge semi truck and trailer ran the stop sign and smacked into the right side of my truck. I ended up in one ditch, and Bessie was thrown into another. I was hurtin' real bad and didn't want to move. But I could hear ol' Bessie moanin' and groanin' from over on the other side of the road. I couldn't see her, but I could tell she was in bad shape just by hearing her groans. Purty soon, a Highway Patrolman came on the scene. He could hear Bessie moanin' and groanin' up a storm, so he went over and checked on her. After he looked at her for a minute, he took out his gun and shot Bessie dead, right between the eyes.

Then, the patrolman walked over to me, looked at me, and said, 'Sir, I'm sorry. Your mule was in such bad shape I had to shoot her. How are *you* feeling?'

"I looked at the gun in his hand, and said, "Just fine, Officer!"

THE BLONDE AND THE PEST

A IR TRAVEL, THESE days, is tough enough without having to put up with a pest seated next to you and be his personal "captive audience" for the next few hours.

Kelly was a bright and attractive, blonde businesswoman, who frequently traveled by air on business. On one such trip, she was seated next to a loud, know-it-all type – a flashy dresser with an expensive suite and a lot of heavy, gold jewelry, who thought he was the life of the party. It was a late flight from New York to Florida, and all Kelly wanted to do was take a nap while the loud guy had, apparently, overdosed on energy drinks. He wanted to play a game.

"I'll ask you a question, and if you don't know the answer, you pay me $5.00, and vice versa," he said.

Kelly declined, and said she just wanted some sleep.

Agitated, the guy persisted. "OK, I get it, you're blonde and probably don't know much, so I'll tell you what: if you don't know the answer, you give me 5 bucks. If you ask me a question that I can't answer, I'll give you 5 *hundred* bucks! How's that?"

Well, this caught Kelly's attention, so she agreed to play one game. He asked the first question: "What is the distance from the earth to the moon?" Kelly didn't know offhand, so she reached into her purse and gave him a $5 bill.

"OK, now it's you turn," he said.

Kelly thought for a few seconds then asked, "What goes up a hill with three legs, and comes down with four legs?" The guy, puzzled, took out his laptop computer and searched for the answer on the Internet while Kelly turned her back to him and took a nap. Frustrated after searching the Internet and even the Library of Congress, the guy even tried sending e-mails to friends and colleagues, to no avail.

Finally, after two hours, Kelly was briefly awakened from her nap by the flashy guy tapping her shoulder. He told her he was unable to come up with the answer to her question, then reached into his wallet, pulled out $500, and gave it to her, begrudgingly admitting defeat. She smiled, thanked him, and quietly put the $500 in her purse.

After a minute or two, the guy, who was more than a little miffed, said, "Well, what's the answer?"

Unable to answer his question, Kelly reached into her purse and, without another word, gave him $5.00, and went back to sleep.

GORILLA ON THE ROOF

THE LITTLE NEIGHBORHOOD had more than its share of excitement that morning. TV News crews were on hand, as were representatives of the City Zoo, a cop or two, neighbors, and various onlookers. Seems that, sometime during the night, a gorilla had escaped from the zoo and, this morning, he was sitting on Tom and Marge's roof. Unfortunately, no one knew exactly how to get a gorilla off of the roof of the average suburban colonial, so someone put in a call to none other than B'wana Ray, former owner and operator of Bwana Ray's GorillaLand (now retired).

An hour or so later, B'wana Ray arrived, looked at the gorilla up on Tom and Marge's roof, returned to his big, old, full-size Econoline van, and brought back a ladder, a baseball bat, a shotgun, and a mean old pit bull.

"What are you going to do?" Tom asked.

"Well," said B'wana Ray, "I'm gonna put this ladder up against your house. Then, I'm gonna climb up onto your roof. Then, I'm gonna knock that there gorilla offa the roof with this here baseball bat. When the gorilla falls off the roof, that there pit bull is specially trained to grab his testicles and not let go. This will subdue the gorilla long enough for me to put him in the cage in the back of my van, take him back to the zoo, and bingo-bango, problem solved!

So, B'wana Ray hoisted the ladder up against the side of the house, positioned the pit bull in an area where he figured the gorilla would land, grabbed the bat and the shotgun, and walked toward the ladder. But, just before he started to climb the ladder, he handed the shotgun to Tom.

Tom, said, "Whoa! What's this shotgun for?"

B'wana Ray spat on the ground and said, "If the gorilla knocks *me* off the roof, shoot the dog!"

GRANDMA'S BOYFRIEND

ONE SUNNY, SATURDAY morning, little 5-year-old Gerald was at his grandmother's house, visiting with her while his Mom and Dad ran some errands. Gerald had brought along some of his toys and was playing with them in Grandma's bedroom while she was dusting.

Out of the blue, Gerald looked up and asked, "Grammy, how come you don't have a boyfriend?"

Not wanting to get into a long, involved explanation, Grandma simply replied, "Honey, my television is my boyfriend. I can sit and watch it all day long downstairs and even up here in my bedroom. The newscasters on TV keep me company. I can watch movies, and I can even watch church services Sunday morning. The comedies make me laugh, and there are shows on every afternoon with stories that I follow. I call them my 'shows.' So, Gerald, I guess you could call my TV my boyfriend."

Gerald seemed satisfied with that explanation, and continued playing. Then, Grandma turned on the old TV in her bedroom. It was an old analog TV with a digital converter Gerald's Dad had installed and a rabbit ears antenna. The reception was bad. Grandma started adjusting the knobs, trying to get the picture in focus. Frustrated, she began hitting the back of the TV, hoping to fix the problem. Sometimes, a good whack made the picture come in.

While Grandma was busy with the TV, the doorbell rang, and little Gerald ran downstairs to answer it. When he opened the door, there stood Father Michael, the Pastor from Grandma's church. He'd stopped by to check on her, as he did with most of the elderly people in his congregation.

"Hello, son," said the priest, "is your grandmother home?"

"Yes, Father," Gerald answered politely, "but she can't come to the door right now. She's up in the bedroom, bangin' her boyfriend!"

Happy Endings

PERFECT FIT

THE OCCASION WAS a crowded dinner at an upscale restaurant. The speaker was Bill Thomson, a veteran financial advisor who had, at great expense, invited the room full of retirees to attend the dinner, which would be followed by his presentation about retirement investment strategies.

But, just before he was about to begin his pitch, Bill bit into a hard roll and cracked his upper dentures. He now looked as if he'd forgotten his teeth! How could he go on?

Turning to the man next to him, Bill said, "My dentures broke. This is awful! I look like I have no teeth!"

The man said, "No problem!" He reached into his pocket and pulled out some false teeth. "Try these," he said.

Desperate to avoid the embarrassment of sending his audience home, or looking totally foolish by trying to speak without teeth, Bill rinsed the dentures in his water glass and tried them on. Unfortunately, they didn't fit. "Too tight," he said.

The man said, "Hmmnn. I have another set. Try these." And gave Bill some different dentures.

Bill tried on the second set of dentures, but they didn't fit, either. "Too loose," said Bill.

Unfazed, the man said, "Don't worry, I have one more set with me." And, pulling them out of his pocket, the man said, "Try these."

Bill did, and to his amazement, they fit perfectly! He rose and made his presentation flawlessly, winning over several new clients. At the end of the evening, Bill went to thank the man who helped him.

"I want to thank you for coming to my aid," said Bill. "Where is your office? I've been looking for a good dentist."

"Oh, you're welcome," the man replied. "But I'm not a dentist, I'm an undertaker!"

HUNGRY MONKEY

Matt walked into the bar with his pet monkey. He ordered a drink, and while he was drinking it, the monkey decided he was hungry. He grabbed some olives from a dish next to the bar and ate them. Then, he swiped some sliced lemons and limes and ate them too. Finally, he jumped onto the pool table, picked up the cue ball and, unbelievably, began pushing it into his mouth. To everyone's absolute amazement, he managed to swallow the entire solid billiard ball!

The bartender screamed at Matt: "Did you see what your monkey did?"

Matt, who was engrossed in conversation with a young lady next to him and missed the whole cue ball incident, said, "No. What?"

The bartender said, "He just ate the cue ball off of my pool table – whole! He just stuck it in his mouth and swallowed the thing!"

"That doesn't surprise me," said Matt. "That damned monkey eats everything in sight. I don't know what to do to stop him. I feed him, so it's not like he's hungry. He was just misbehaving. Look, I'm sorry. I like this place and want to come back. So, I'll pay for everything he ate." Matt paid the bartender for his drink and for everything the monkey ate, and left.

Two weeks later, Matt returned to the bar with the monkey. Matt ordered a drink, and while he was drinking it, his monkey started running around again. But, this time, he wasn't eating everything in sight. Finally, the monkey picked up a maraschino cherry, stuck it in his butt, pulled it back out, and ate it as the bar's disgusted customers watched.

The bartender went ballistic. "Did you see what your monkey did just now?" he shouted.

"No," said Matt. "*Now* what?"

"He stuck a maraschino cherry up his ass, then pulled it out and ate it in front of all my customers! This ain't the zoo here, bro!"

"Sorry," said Matt, "but it doesn't surprise me. He still eats everything in sight, but ever since that time he swallowed your cue ball, he measures everything first!"

STOPPED FOR SPEEDING

After years of hard work, Marty finally rewarded himself by buying that Ferrari he always wanted. He was cruising along the interstate one summer evening, enjoying a nice drive with the top down, on an open stretch of highway. There was no traffic visible for miles, so he decided to open it up and see what his Ferrari could do.

As the speedometer passed 90, he suddenly saw flashing red and blue lights behind him.

"Aw, come on. There's no traffic out here, and I'm not endangering anyone," Marty said to himself. "Where did that cop come from, anyway?"

Deciding that there was no way a police cruiser could catch up to a Ferrari, Marty pushed his speed up to 100…then 120…then realized, "what am I doing?" He immediately began to slow down, then pulled over, stopped, and waited for the highway patrolman.

The cop stopped behind him, slowly walked up to him, took his license and registration without a word, and examined them and the car. He went back to his patrol car, to make sure the Ferrari wasn't stolen, and saw that Marty had no outstanding tickets. Then, he returned to the Ferrari and said to Marty, "Sir, you were traveling at a high rate of speed. But it's been a long day. This is the end of my shift. It's Friday, and I don't feel like doing any more paperwork. You don't have any outstanding citations against you, so I'll tell you what. If you can give me an excuse for the way you were driving that I haven't heard before, I'll let you off with just a warning."

Marty thought for a minute or two, and said, "Last week, my wife ran off with a cop. When I saw your flashing lights coming up behind me, I was afraid you were trying to give her back!"

The officer said, "Have a nice weekend."

THE PARROT

Anne always wanted a parrot. One day, she was walking past a pet shop and immediately spotted the bird of her dreams: a large, beautiful, multi-colored parrot, with a sign on the cage that said: SPECIAL SALE: $50.

Anne rushed inside, and asked the pet shop owner why the price was so low for such a magnificent bird.

The owner looked around guiltily, then looked at her rather bashfully, then hesitantly said, "Look, ma'am. I've gotta tell you, this bird used to live in a house of prostitution, and sometimes says some pretty off-color stuff. It could be embarrassing."

Anne gave this some thought, but it was a splendid bird, and exactly the type of bird she'd always been looking for. She decided to take it.

Anne brought the parrot home, hung the bird's cage in the living room, and waited for it to say something. The bird looked around the room, looked at Anne, and said, "New house, new madam."

Anne blushed and was rather offended at the implication but knew where the parrot was raised and thought, "Hey, that's not so bad…"

Then, Anne's two teen-age daughters Lindsay and Leah came home from school. The bird looked at them and said, "New house, new madam, new girls."

Lindsay and Leah were a bit shocked, but when Anne explained where the parrot had come from, they thought it was actually kind of cute, and the three women began to laugh about the situation.

Moments later, Anne's husband, Keith, came home from work.

And the bird looked at him and said, "Hi, Keith!"

JOB QUALIFICATIONS

IN TODAY'S ECONOMY, it is becoming more and more difficult to keep a job, particularly blue collar manufacturing jobs.

Stan and Zigmund were close friends. Both were immigrants who came to America with their parents when they were youngsters when their eastern European country was embroiled in a terrible civil war. Both Stan and Zig learned English from watching TV and simply by living day-by-day in America. They did everything together. They even became U.S. citizens together.

But, now, both Stan and Zig were laid off, and after trying to find work for a few weeks, they decided to go to the unemployment office.

When the clerk asked Stan his occupation, he said, "Garment Stitcher. Down at da plant, I used to sew da elastic into da women's cotton panties."

The clerk looked up Stan's occupation in her computer to determine the size of each unemployment insurance check Stan would receive. She found Stan's job classified as "unskilled labor," and told him each of his unemployment checks would be $300.

Then the clerk asked Zig his occupation, and Zig answered Diesel Fitter.

The clerk looked up Zig's job and found that it was considered "skilled labor," qualifying him for $600 checks.

When Stan found out Zigmund's checks were going to be twice as big as his, he stormed back into the clerk's office and demanded to know why.

The clerk said, "Simple. Garment Stitchers are considered unskilled labor, and Diesel Fitters are classified as skilled labor."

"What skill?" Stan yelled. "I sew da elastic onto women's panties. Zig looks at da size, puts da panties over his head, and says, "Yah, diesel fitter!"

FUSSIN' AN' A-FEUDIN'

RUFUS AND CLARENCE were two ornery old cusses who lived in the backwoods of the Ozarks. Both were in their 60s now, and they hated each other. In fact, they had been feuding most their lives, although it was probably a good bet that neither of them remembered why.

Fortunately, Rufus and Clarence lived on opposite sides of a river that was deep and wide enough for boat traffic, barges and commerce, but narrow enough for the two loudmouths to yell threats at each other. Every morning, just after sun-up, both of the old geezers would go down to their respective sides of the river and shout across at each other.

"Rufus!" Clarence would shout, "Y'all better thank yore lucky stars I cain't swim, else I'd swim 'crost this here river and whup yore scrawny bee-hind!"

"Clarence," Rufus would answer, "you ol' barge butt! You better be thankin' YORE lucky stars I cain't swim neither, er I'd come across an' open up a can o' whup-ass on Y'ALL!

This went on virtually every morning for more than 20 years, even after the Army Corps of Engineers had built a bridge across the river, a half-mile downstream. Apparently, neither of the feuders wanted to waste energy they'd need for a good fistfight on a lot of walkin' and river crossin'. So, it went on. Every morning, every day, for five years after the bridge had been built.

But, finally, Rufus's wife had had enough. "Rufus," she hollered one day, "I cain't take it no more! This constant hootin' an' a-hollerin', fussin' an' a-feudin' with Clarence is drivin' me plumb squirrely! If'n yore so dad-blamed set on whuppin' Clarence's bee-hind, y'all best git yore lazy butt 'cross that there bridge and have at it!"

Rufus thought for a minute, chewed on his terbacky for a minute, scratched his fanny for a minute, then said, "Yore raht, woman! I'm a-gonna cross that there bridge and whup ol' Clarence's nasty butt!"

So, Rufus walked out the door, down to the river, along the riverbank, and to the bridge. On the side of the bridge, about halfway across, there was a sign posted but, from the riverbank, Rufus couldn't quite make out what it said. In fact, Rufus wasn't much of a reader anyway – he considered 6th Grade his Senior Year!

So, Rufus started across the bridge, mumbling, "Ahm comin' t'getcha Clarence, ya varmint!"

Halfway across, he leaned over the side, and read the sign that was posted on the bridge. He stood up straight, rubbed his eyes, leaned over the side, and read the sign again, just to make sure his eyes weren't foolin' him.

Then, he jumped up with a "whoop!" He spun around, turned back toward his side of the river and ran home, screaming. He raced into the house, slammed the door, and ran to the windows, slamming each one shut and locking it. Then, he grabbed his shotgun and dove behind the bed, where he knelt, puffing, panting, and sweating.

"Rufus!" cried his missus, "What in tarnation has got into you? Is there a bear after ya, er sumthin'? I thought you wuz gonna go whup ol' Clarence's butt!"

"I was, woman, I was!" shouted Rufus.

"Well, then, whut, pray tell, are ya doin', hidin' behind the bed?"

"Well," muttered the terror-stricken Rufus, "I went to the bridge and started acrost it, but then I stopped to read the sign hung there on the bridge, halfway acrost."

"And," his wife said, "whut did the sign say?"

"The sign," Rufus continued, "said Clearance, 13 feet 6 inches! He ain't NEVER looked THAT big from OUR side of the river!"

LUCK OF THE IRISH

O'BRIEN WAS RUMMAGING around in an old barn when – faith and begorrah! – he discovered a leprechaun hiding in the corner.

"Ah, O'Brien, it's your lucky day," said the leprechaun. "Ye found me, fair and square, so I now must grant you three wishes. What'll it be?"

Now, the amazed O'Brien certainly loved his Guinness, and after scratching his head awhile, he couldn't think of anything more pleasant than a bottle of Guinness that never gets empty. So, that was his first wish: "I'd like a bottle of Guinness that never gets empty," O'Brien told the leprechaun.

"Granted!" said the leprechaun, and he produced the magic bottle of O'Brien's favorite drink. "When you can think of what you want for your other two wishes, you'll know where to find me!" And the leprechaun climbed back into the corner, behind some rags and tools.

O'Brien was delighted, to say the least! He got drunk on his one bottle of Guinness every day for weeks. Life was wonderful!

A month later, O'Brien had been having such a great time that he'd almost completely forgotten about the leprechaun. But now, in what he considered a brilliant stroke of genius, O'Brien determined exactly what his two other wishes would be. He went back to the old barn, and found the leprechaun hiding in his corner.

"All right, O'Brien," said the impertinent little leprechaun. "You have two more wishes. What do you want?"

O'Brien put on his craftiest grin, rubbed his hands together, and said, "You know that magic, never-ending bottle of Guinness you gave me before?"

"Of course," said the leprechaun.

"Well, for my final two wishes," said O'Brien, "I'd like two *more* of 'em!"

ALL ABOARD!

MOM WAS WORKING in the kitchen, listening to Bryan, her little, 5-year-old son, playing with his new toy train set in the family room.

She heard the train stop, then heard her son say, "All of you bastards who want to get off, get the hell off now, 'cuz this is the last stop! And all of you sons of bitches who are getting on, get your asses in the train NOW, 'cuz we're headed down the track!"

Mom was shocked and horrified at her son's salty language! She rushed into the family room and told Bryan, "We don't use that kind of language in this house, young man! Now, I want you to go to your room THIS MINUTE, and STAY there for TWO HOURS. You just sit there and think about the words you used that you will NEVER use under this roof again. When you come out, you may play with your train, but ONLY if you use the proper language!"

Two hours later, little Bryan came, sheepishly, out of his bedroom, and resumed playing with his train.

Soon, Mom heard the train come to a stop, and she heard her son say, in a courteous, "official"-sounding voice, like that of a train conductor: "Ladies and gentlemen, your attention please. We would like to welcome all passengers to Bryantown. Please remember to take all of your personal belongings with you as you leave the train. Thank you, for using Bryan's Railroad. We hope your trip was a pleasant one, and that you will ride with us again."

Mom beamed, pleased that she was able to teach her young son a valuable lesson.

Little Bryan continued, "For those of you just boarding, please remember there is no smoking on the train. We hope you will have a pleasant and relaxing journey with us today."

And, just as Mom was about to commend her son on his

wonderful behavior, the child added in his "official" voice: "For those of you who are pissed off about the TWO HOUR DELAY, please see the bitch in the kitchen!"

ROUGH NIGHT

FRED WAS A regular at a friendly bar in his neighborhood, conveniently located down at the end of his block. He was there most nights. But, one night, he drank quite a bit more than usual.

Just before 2:00 AM, the bartender announced last call, and Fred decided he'd had enough. But, as he stood up to leave, even Fred realized that, this time, he may have been "over-served" even more than usual. He couldn't even stand – in fact, he fell flat on his face!

Although there weren't many bar patrons left, Fred was too embarrassed to draw even more attention to himself, so he quietly crawled out of the bar, so no one would see just how plastered he was. When he got outside, Fred thought the air would revive him a bit, but he was wrong.

He leaned on the outside wall of the bar, but just couldn't get his wobbly legs to support him. "Thank God I didn't drive tonight," Fred said to himself, "I'm shurtinly in no condi-condi-condishun to drive home!" With that, Fred crawled home, grateful that he lived less than a block away.

When he got home, he crawled through the door and into his bedroom, where he pulled himself up onto the bed, and fell asleep fully clothed.

The next morning, Fred was awakened by his wife, standing over him and shouting.

"Well, Fred," she said, "you really did it this time! You managed to get more crocked than ever before!"

Fred was a bit offended. "What makes you say that?" he said, "just because I fell asleep with my clothes on?"

"No, Fred," said his wife. "I'm saying that because the bar called this morning. You left without your wheelchair again!"

THE BOY IN THE CLOSET

LIFE IN THE suburbs can sometimes rival life as it is portrayed on soap operas. In this case, a bored, stay-at-home suburban Mom took a lover during the day while her husband was at work. Without her knowledge, the woman's 9-year-old son was hiding in her bedroom closet that day.

Suddenly and unexpectedly, her husband came home, so she hid her lover in the closet. The boy now had company.

Boy: "Dark in here."

Man: "Yes, it is."

Boy: "I have a baseball."

Man: "That's nice."

Boy: "Want to buy it?"

Man: "No, thanks."

Boy: "My Dad's outside."

Man: "OK, kid. How much?"

Boy: "$250."

The man paid up and became the proud owner of an expensive baseball.

A week later, it happened again. Suddenly, the boy and his Mom's lover found themselves in the closet together.

Boy: "Dark in here."

Man: "Yes, it is."

Boy: "I have a baseball glove."

Man: "How much?"

Boy: "$750."

Man: "Fine."

A few days later, the boy and his Dad are sitting in the family room when the father said to the boy, "Grab your glove and baseball, son. I'll get a bat and hit some to ya!"

The boy said, "I can't Dad. I sold them."

"Sold them?" his Dad said. "That's weird. How much did you sell them for?"

The son says, "$1,000."

The father says, "Son, I admire your salesmanship, but that's way more than those things are worth. You shouldn't take advantage of your friends and overcharge them like that! I'm going to take you to church, and you're going to confess!"

It was Saturday, so the father and son went to church, where the priest was hearing Confession. The Dad put the 9-year-old boy in the confessional, closed the door, and sat down in a nearby pew.

The boy said, "Dark in here."

The priest said, "Don't start *that* shit again!"

AMAZING MEDICINE

HARRY WAS GETTING along in years, while his wife Joyce was several years younger. Alas, one day Harry discovered he was unable to perform sexually.

He went to his urologist, who prescribed the Little Blue Pill for his erectile dysfunction. But it didn't work for Harry. All the pill did was give everything he looked at a bluish hue.

The doctor then prescribed the other two popular ED pills, but neither of those worked for Harry either, and he was reluctant to try weird appliances or scary injections. Finally, as a last resort, the urologist referred Harry to an American Indian Medicine Man he'd heard about.

In desperation – and with nothing left to lose – Harry visited the Medicine Man.

The old Indian began chanting and proceeded to mix some powders, herbs, and leaves together. He then threw some of the mixture into a flame. There was a flash and a loud "poof," followed by billowing blue smoke.

The Medicine Man then put the mixture into a bottle and said, "This powerful medicine. Mix with juice from agave cactus, and drink when ready for sex. Then, just before sex, to make medicine work, just say out loud, '1-2-3!' Penis will rise at once and be strong all night or for many moons – as long as you want! Medicine very strong but work only one time a year."

Harry said, "What happens when my wife and I have had enough, and we just don't want to continue any longer?"

The Medicine Man replied, "Just have wife say '1-2-3-4,' and erection go down immediately. But, be warned: you cannot use medicine again for another year!"

"That's a long time," Harry said, trying to control his excitement, "but it shouldn't be a problem."

Harry rushed home, eager to try out his new powers and prowess. That night, he decided to surprise Joyce. He showered, shaved, put on his best cologne, and drank the medicine. Then, he climbed into bed and, lying behind her, said, "1-2-3!" Amazingly, Harry suddenly became more wonderfully aroused than ever before in his life, just as the Medicine Man had promised!

And Joyce rolled over and asked, "What did you say '1-2-3' for?"

THE WORLD'S BEST HUSBAND

SEVERAL MEN WERE in the locker room of the local Country Club, toweling-off after their shower.

A cell phone on a bench rang, and Frank reached over, engaged the hands-free function, and answered, "Hello?"

Because the speaker phone was on, everyone in the room quieted down and listened as a woman's cheerful voice said, "Hi, Sweetie! Are you at the club?"

Frank answered, "Yes, I am!"

"Well, I'm at Neiman-Marcus, Honey, and they've got this beautiful, lightweight leather coat on sale, right now, for only $2,000. Is it OK if I buy it? Please dear?"

"Sure. Go ahead, if you like it that much."

"I also stopped by the BMW dealership earlier, she continued, "and I drove that new 650 convertible. It's sooo beautiful, and they have the red one with the tan interior I just love."

"How much?" asked Frank.

"$90,000."

"OK," said Frank, "but make sure that covers everything – taxes, delivery, everything."

"Oh, thank you, dear! And one more thing: I was just talking to Carla the realtor, and she said the house I wanted last year is back on the market. Now they're asking just $980,000 for it!"

"Well, go ahead and make an offer of $900,000 for it," said Frank. "They'll probably go for it. If they don't, we'll just pay the extra $80,000 if that's the house you really want!"

"Wow! OK, Honey! Thanks! I'll see you later! I love you so so much!"

"Bye, now," said Frank. "I love you too!" And he reached over and ended the call.

The other men in the locker room stared in astonishment, their mouths wide open.

Then, Frank picked up the cell phone and asked, "Anyone know whose phone this is?"

PATIENT PATIENT

R ALPH'S STORY WILL, no doubt, strike close to home for anyone affected by the increasing cost of health care. It seems that more and more doctors are running their offices impersonally, like an assembly line. In an effort to be more efficient, they are often less efficient. Witness Ralph's situation:

Ralph had shingles. He walked into the doctor's office and up to the receptionist's desk.

"What do you have?" asked the receptionist.

"Shingles," Ralph replied.

"Is this your first time here?" she inquired.

"Yes," answered Ralph.

"Then write your name, address, phone number, and the name of your health care insurance here, have a seat over there, complete this questionnaire, and one of the nurses will call your name," said the receptionist.

Ralph wrote down the information, sat down in the reception room, and began filling out the doctor's questionnaire.

Twenty minutes later, a nurse's aide came out and asked Ralph what he had.

"Shingles," replied Ralph.

So, she brought Ralph inside, took down his weight and height, gave him a blood pressure test, and took his temperature. She then directed him to an examination room and asked him to wait for the doctor.

A half-hour later, the doctor appeared and asked Ralph, "What do you have?"

"Shingles," Ralph replied.

"Where?" asked the doctor, quickly examining Ralph's exposed neck and arms.

"Outside on the truck," said Ralph. "Where do you want me to unload 'em?"

SUNDAY SCHOOL

THE PASTOR STOOD in front of his congregation one Sunday, and announced: "For those of you who have children and don't know it, we have a Sunday School downstairs."

Later, downstairs, one of the Sunday School teachers was working with her group of preschoolers. She was concerned that her students might be a little confused about Jesus Christ, because at their early age, all that most of them really knew about Jesus was that He was born on Christmas Day, which was a wonderful time of year for them. She wanted to make sure they understood that He grew up, performed miracles, preached, died for our sins, went to Heaven, and so forth.

As part of her lesson that day, the Sunday School teacher asked her class, "Where is Jesus today?"

Cameron raised his hand and said, "He's in Heaven!"

Lauren was called on, and she said, "He's in my heart."

While other children offered similar insightful comments, little Kelly was waving her hand furiously for attention, hoping that someone else wouldn't come up with her answer before she could. Finally, unable to wait any longer, she blurted out, "I know! I know! Jesus is in our bathroom!"

The whole Sunday School class got very quiet, looked at the teacher, and waited for a response. The teacher was completely at a loss for a few very long seconds. Finally, she gathered her wits and asked little Kelly how she knew this.

And little Kelly said, "Well, every morning my Daddy comes out of his bedroom, bangs on the bathroom door, and yells, 'Jesus Christ, are you still in there?'"

SHIRLEY

6 0-YEAR-OLD SHIRLEY WAS the neighborhood busy-body. She knew everything about everyone, memorized every rule the Subdivision Association had, and had no qualms about citing those rules to offenders, and spent her days policing the neighborhood and "visiting" neighbors.

Late one afternoon, while her husband was still at work, Shirley casually dropped in, unannounced, at the home of a young couple who'd recently moved next door. Shirley rang the doorbell, opened the front door, and boldly walked in, saying "Knock knock!"

There, lying on the couch, totally naked, was her young, attractive neighbor, Erin. Soft music was playing, candles were lit, and the aroma of jasmine perfume filled the room.

"What are you doing?" said the shocked Shirley.

Showing no embarrassment at her nosy neighbor's rude intrusion, Erin answered, "I'm waiting for Jerry, my husband, to come home from work."

"But you're naked!" Shirley remarked loudly.

"This is what we call my love dress," Erin explained.

"But you're naked!" the flabbergasted Shirley said again.

"Jerry loves when I surprise him this way," said Erin. "When he comes home and sees me, he instantly becomes romantic, and we make love for hours. He can't get enough of me!"

Shirley had heard enough. Maybe this was how she could re-ignite the spark in her marriage with Sam, who was nearing retirement and never seemed interested in her any more. She went home, undressed, showered, put on her best cologne, dimmed the lights, lit some candles, put on some romantic music, and reclined on the couch, waiting for Sam to come home.

Soon he arrived. He walked in, saw Shirley posed provocatively on the couch, and said, "What are you doing?"

"This is my love dress," Shirley whispered sensually.

"Needs ironing!" said Sam.

TRAVELING WITH THE POPE

Pope Benedict's driver had just finished loading all of the Pope's luggage into his limousine, and they were ready for a leisurely drive from the airport to the Vatican. Then, he noticed that the Pope had remained standing outside of the limo with a forlorn look on his face.

"What is wrong, Your Holiness?" asked the driver.

"When I was a young man in Germany, there was nothing I enjoyed more than to get behind the wheel of a Mercedes or BMW and drive down the Autobahn," said the Pope. "When I was a Cardinal, I drove as often as I could. But now, they don't let me. I would like to drive."

Although the driver tried to resist, fearing an accident or surely the loss of his job, there was no denying the wishes of the Holy Father. So, he climbed into the back of the limousine, and Pope Benedict happily took the wheel. But soon, the driver regretted not taking a stronger stance. Because no sooner had they left the airport, than they were barreling down the freeway, approaching 145 kilometers per hour – more than 90 miles an hour!

"Please slow down, Your Holiness!" the driver shouted from the back seat.

But there was no deterring the German Pope, who had routinely driven the Autobahn at speeds exceeding 100 mph – the speed they were going when they passed a PolStrada motorcycle, one of the highway patrolmen charged with policing Italy's autostrada, or motorways. He immediately turned on his siren, pursued the limo, and pulled it over.

The driver knew that he would certainly lose his license and his job. He sat quietly in the back of the limousine as the Pope rolled down the window.

The police officer approached the limo and immediately recognized none other than the Pope behind the wheel! He quickly glanced into the back seat and saw a well-dressed man in black who sat there quietly. Without a word to either of them, the cop hurried back to his motorcycle, and got on the radio.

"I need to talk to the Chief," he told the dispatcher.

The Police Chief got on the radio, and the motorcycle cop told him he'd just stopped a limousine doing 169 kilometers per hour – over 105 miles an hour – far in excess of the speed limit.

"So, what's the problem? Give him a ticket!" said the Chief.

"I don't think we want to do that. This guy's really important," said the cop.

"Hey, just because he's riding in a limo doesn't mean he's above the law," said the Chief.

"But this guy is really *really* important!" insisted the cop.

"Who do you have there, the Mayor?" said the Chief.

"Bigger," said the cop.

"The Prime Minister?" said the Chief.

"Bigger," said the cop.

"Well," said the Chief, "who is it?"

The cop said, "I think it's God Himself!"

The Chief, now thinking that the cop must have fallen off his motorcycle without his helmet on, said, "What makes you think the passenger in that limousine is God?"

The cop said, "He's got the Pope as His chauffeur!"

MARBLE RYE

Sid and Hymie were a couple of old, retired, Jewish pals. Sid was 68 and Hymie was 70. They were sitting together on their usual park bench one morning, and Hymie had just finished his morning jog. At the age of 70, he wasn't even out of breath!

"Hymie," said Sid, "you've gotta tell me. Every morning, for years now, you go jogging, and you're not even short of breath. You're in terrific shape. I try to watch my weight, walk every day, watch what I eat, yadda-yadda-yadda, and I don't have nearly as much energy as you. And as far as the women are concerned…forget about it! What's your secret?"

"Well," said Hymie, "I don't know why no one ever asked me this before, but you know Finkelstein's bakery on Elm Street? They've got this marble rye bread that's sensational! I eat some marble rye from that bakery every day. It keeps my energy up, and – now, get *this*, Sid – it's like Viagra! It gives me tremendous stamina with the ladies. I could have sex for an hour!"

"Oy! An *hour* you say? *This* I've gotta try!" said Sid.

So, on the way home, Sid stopped at the bakery, and asked the woman behind the counter, "Do you have any marble rye bread?"

"Do we?" she said. "That whole shelf back there is filled with loaves of marble rye! Do you want some?"

Thinking that the bread might make for a big weekend for him with the ladies, Sid said, "I'll take five loaves!"

The clerk said, "My goodness! Five loaves! Don't you think that, before you even get to the *third* loaf, it'll be *hard?*"

And Sid said, "I can't believe it! Everybody in the *world* knew about this marble rye bread thing but *me!*"

CONSEQUENCES

Jack decided to go skiing with his buddy Bob. So they loaded up Jack's minivan and headed north to a remote ski area they'd never been to before. After they had been driving for hours on back roads, darkness fell, and they suddenly found themselves caught in a terrible blizzard in the middle of nowhere. Finally, they pulled into a nearby farm and asked the attractive woman who answered the door if they could spend the night.

"I realize it's terrible weather out there, and I have this huge house all to myself, but I'm recently widowed," she said. "I'm afraid the neighbors will talk if I let you stay in my house."

"Don't worry," Jack said, "We'll be happy to sleep in the barn. And if the weather breaks, we'll be gone at first light."

The lady agreed. Jack and Bob found their way to the barn and settled in for the night. Come morning, the weather had cleared, and they got on their way. The two buddies enjoyed a great weekend of skiing.

But, about nine months later, Jack got an unexpected letter from an attorney. It took him a few minutes to figure it out, but he finally determined that it was from the attorney of the attractive widow in whose barn he and Bob had slept on the ski weekend.

Jack dropped in on his friend, and asked, "Bob, do you remember that good-looking widow from the farm we stayed at on our ski holiday up north about 9 months ago?"

"Yes…of course I do," said Bob, hesitantly.

"Did you, uh, happen to get up in the middle of the night, go up to the house and pay her a visit?" asked Jack.

"Well, um, yes," Bob said, a little embarrassed about being discovered, "I have to admit that I did."

"And did you have sex?" asked Jack

"Well, yeah...I admit I did go up to the house and have sex with the widow. Can you blame me? She was gorgeous!" said Bob.

"But, Bob, did you happen to use *my* name instead of telling her your own name?" asked Jack.

Now, Bob's face turned crimson red, and he said, "Yeah, look, I'm sorry, buddy. I'm afraid I did tell her I was you. Uh, but why, Jack, are you asking me...now...about something that happened nine months ago?"

Jack said, "She just died and left me a huge fortune!"

CHINESE NEWLYWEDS

C HEN AND LIN were two Chinese kids who, while in their teens, immigrated to San Francisco with their parents. Chen's parents started an authentic Chinese restaurant, and Lin's parents opened a successful gift shop in San Francisco's popular Chinatown.

Chen and Lin met and fell in love. They dated for a couple of years under the watchful eyes of their parents, who strictly forbade any hanky-panky. So, when they eventually got married, Lin was a virgin, and Chen wasn't all that experienced himself.

Their wedding was a joyous affair with a reception held at Chen's parents' restaurant, where Chen had begun a career as a skilled waiter.

On their wedding night, Lin cowered, naked, under the sheets while Chen undressed. He climbed into bed next to her and tried to be reassuring.

"My darring," he said, "I know dis first time for you, an' you velly flighten. But we have velly long life ahead of us, and I wish velly much to prease you.

Lin nodded her head rapidly with the sheets pulled up to her chin.

Chen continued: "I plomise you, I give you anyting you want tonight, to make you feer at ease. I do anyting – juss anyting you want. Wha you want?"

A thoughtful silence followed, while Lin considered what sexual favors she had ever even *heard* about, from her friends, from magazines, from movies, and in school. Chen waited patiently and eagerly for her response.

Finally, Lin replied in a shy, quiet voice, "Chen, I wanna try somethin' I hear about from flends in-a school. I wanna try '69'!"

Another thoughtful silence followed as Chen considered Lin's request. Eventually, in a puzzled tone, he said, "You wanna try Chicken wiff Broccori?"

WORLD'S FASTEST GOAT

Ronnie and Junior were out a-huntin' in the hills of Kentucky when they came upon a huge hole in the ground. They looked down into the hole and were amazed at the depth of it.

Ronnie said, "Whoo-ee! That there's some hole! I cain't even see the bottom! Ah wonder how deep it is."

Junior said, "Ya got me – I don't know. Say, look here: let's throw somethin' big down into that there hole and lissen, an' see how long it takes to hit bottom!"

Ronnie said, "Hey, good idee, Junior! There's a old, rusty transmission just a-settin' here. Gimme a hand, and we'll chuck 'er in the hole an' see!"

So, Ronnie and Junior picked up the transmission, carried it over to the hole, counted one-two-three while swinging it back and forth, and chucked it into the hole. They watched it drop out of sight, and stood there, listening and looking over the edge of the hole, when they suddenly heard a loud rustling in the brush behind them. They turned around just in time to see one of the scariest sights they'd ever seen: a goat was a-coming straight at them at an amazing speed! In all their born days, neither of the boys had ever seen a goat run that fast! The goat raced right up to the hole, and without a moment's hesitation, jumped right in, head first.

Ronnie and Junior just stood there, looking down into the hole, wondering what just happened when they heard another rustling in the brush behind them. But, this time, it was just an old farmer.

"Say there," said the farmer. "You fellers didn't happen to see my goat 'round here anywhere, didja?"

And Ronnie said, "Funny you should ask! We was just a-standin' here a minute ago, and we seen the world's fastest goat come a-runnin' outa them there bushes like the devil hisself was after him. He just missed us an' jumped head-first into this here hole!"

The farmer said, "Nope, guess it weren't my goat. I had mine chained to a transmission!"

ONE LAST FLING

MAURY AND LEO were two old friends: widowers, who were getting on in years. So, they decided to have a night on the town – one last fling – while they were still able.

They started the evening at their favorite bar, and had more than a few drinks. In fact, both Maury and Leo were three sheets to the wind as they left the bar and headed for a local brothel late that night.

When they got to the bordello, the Madam took one look at the two drunken, old geezers, neither of whom could see very well even when they were sober and whispered to her Manager: "Go up to the first two bedrooms, and put an inflated doll in each bed. These two are so old and drunk that I'm not even gonna waste two of my girls on them. They won't know the difference."

The Manager did as he was told, and the Madam escorted Maury and Leo upstairs to the first two bedrooms. Each of them entered his room and took care of business in no time at all.

As they were walking home, neither Maury nor Leo were pleased with their "final fling" experience. Maury said, "You know, Leo, I think my girl was dead or passed out on drugs."

"Why do you say that?" asked Leo.

"Well, she never moved or even made a sound. All the time I was making sweet love to her. And she even felt kind of clammy!" said Maury.

"Huh!" said Leo. "Well, it couldn't have been worse than *my* experience. I think my girl was a damned witch!"

"A witch!?" said Maury, "Why would you say that?"

"Well," said Leo, "I was making love to her, kissing her on the neck, and I gave her a little bite. She farted, flew out the window, and took my teeth with her!"

MURPHY'S LATE ARRIVAL

IT WAS 3:00 AM, and Murphy was finally getting home after a long evening and too many pints of Guinness at the pub. Murphy's wife expected him to be home by midnight, so he knew there would be trouble on the home front unless he could convince her he'd come home at a more respectable hour. His wife usually turned in around 11:00 PM, so Murphy knew he had a chance of succeeding.

As Murphy quietly opened his front door, he was totally feeling no pain whatsoever. His wife was asleep! All he had to do was sneak upstairs as silently as possible and climb into bed. If she awoke, he could always pretend he was just coming back from the loo.

But, just as he was about to begin climbing the stairs, he heard the large cuckoo clock in the hallway go off, with the bird cuckooing three times!

"Shite!" Murphy said under his breath, and thinking as quickly as his stewed brain would allow, Murphy cuckooed an additional nine times, imitating the bird perfectly! Anyone who'd been listening would swear the clock just cuckooed 12 times, and it was midnight.

The talented mimick felt pretty proud of himself. He crept silently up the stairs, undressed, slipped into bed, and immediately began sleeping the sleep of the innocent.

The next morning, Murphy's wife casually asked him what time he'd gotten home the night before.

"Uh…I believe 'twas 12 o'clock, m'luv," he answered. "Why?"

"Then I think we'll have to get that cuckoo clock fixed," she said.

"Why?" he asked.

"Well," she said, "late last night, it cuckooed three times, said 'Shite!', cuckooed three more times, cleared its throat, cuckooed two more times, chuckled, cuckooed twice more, belched, cuckooed two last times, and farted!"

SHARING

THE SCENE WAS the neighborhood McDonald's. And the story that was unfolding was a tender tale of loving and sharing.

The old man placed an order for one hamburger, a small order of french fries, and a coffee. He carefully carried the order to a table in the corner, where his wife, a small woman with gray hair, awaited his arrival, with napkins, a packet of sugar, and a stir stick.

When the old man arrived at the table, with shaky hands he carefully counted out the french fries, dividing them into two piles on the napkins his wife had set out. Meanwhile, she opened the small packet of sugar, emptied it into the coffee, and stirred it with the plastic stir stick. She took a sip of the coffee then he took a sip, and set the cup down between them.

As he began to eat his few bites of hamburger, the people around them were looking over and whispering. They were thinking: That poor old couple. All they can afford is one meal between them, yet they seem to be sharing it so routinely and lovingly.

As the man began to eat his fries, a young man walked up to their table and politely offered to buy another meal for the elderly couple. The old man said, "No, we're fine. We're used to sharing everything."

People closer to the table noticed that the little old lady still hadn't eaten a bite. She sat there patiently, watching her husband eat, occasionally taking a sip of their shared coffee.

Again, the young man came over and begged them to let him buy them a second meal. This time, the old woman said, "No thank you, dearie, we're used to sharing everything."

Finally, as the old man finished and was wiping his face neatly with the napkin, the young man again came over to the little old lady, who had yet to eat a single bite of food, and said, "Ma'am, your husband appears to be finished. What are you waiting for?"

And she answered, "The teeth!"

THE HORTH WHITHPERER

BEN WAS A rancher – a horse breeder – in Arizona. Unfortunately, because he spent most of his time around horses, Ben had little patience with people. One day, a friend phoned Ben and said he wanted to send over someone who was interested in buying a horse.

Ben agreed reluctantly and asked, "How will I recognize him?"

His friend said, "Well, that's easy. He's a former jockey – just a little guy – and he has a speech impediment."

The ex-jockey arrived, and Ben asked him if he was looking for a colt (young male horse), or a filly (young female horse).

"I'd like to thee a filly," said the ex-jockey.

Right off the bat, the little guy and his speech impediment kinda rubbed Ben the wrong way, but the rancher showed him a prized filly.

"Nithe lookin' horth, said the jockey. "Can you give me a boothst up, tho I can look at her eyeth?"

Gritting his teeth, Ben picked up the little guy, who gave the horse's eyes the once over.

"Nithe eyeth. Can I thee her earzth?"

Now, the rancher was getting a bit tired of lifting the height-challenged jockey, but he picked up the little fella again and showed him the horse's ears.

"Nithe earzth. Can I see her mouf?"

By now, Ben was getting pretty ticked off, because the little guy insisted on attending to every little detail, although he didn't seem to know quite what he was looking for. Worse yet, he felt no qualms about having the rancher lift him up, again and again, like some sort of servant. But, Ben took a calming breath, picked up the jockey again, and showed him the horse's mouth.

"Nice mouf. Can I thee her twat?" said the little guy, boldly.

Well, that was the last straw! *"Not only is he talkin' filthy, now,"* Ben said to himself, *"But what does he think I am – some kinda freakin' veterinarian gynecologist?"* Mad as fire at this point, the big rancher grabbed the ex-jockey under his arms, lifted the little guy up, and rammed his head as far as it would go up the horse's fanny! He then pulled him out and slammed him to the ground.

The jockey got up, sputtering and coughing, and said, "Perhapth I should wephwase that. Can I thee her wun awound a widdle bit?"

THE PICKLE SLICER INCIDENT

RICHARD WORKED IN a pickle packing plant. Having grown up in the days of punk rock, Richard had more than his share of tattoos and piercings although they didn't detract from his appearance or from the quality of his work, packing pickles into jars.

But Richard also had a problem, for which he was seeking professional help. For many years, Richard had the curious, powerful urge to put his penis into the pickle slicer at the plant. The urge was so strong that he couldn't sleep most nights, hence the need for psychiatric help.

After six months of sessions, his therapist gave up. Against his better judgment, he advised Richard to go ahead and do it, or he would never have peace of mind.

Several days later, Richard came home from work early with a pained look on his face. His wife Donna became alarmed and wanted to know what happened.

Richard tearfully confessed his tormenting, long-term desire to put his penis in the pickle slicer. He went on to explain how he secretly went to a therapist for months, to no avail. Then, he explained that he finally went ahead and did it and, as a result, he had been fired from his job.

Donna gasped and ran over to her husband. She knew he had a high threshold of pain, what with the piercings, tattoos and all, but she couldn't understand how Richard could possibly even be standing there if he'd put his penis into the pickle slicer at work earlier that day. She quickly yanked down his pants and boxer shorts, only to find a normal, completely intact penis.

Looking up, Donna said, "Richard, I don't understand. What happened with the pickle slicer?"

Richard said, "She got fired, too."

ELLEN'S VACATION IN ROME

ELLEN WAS AT the salon, getting her hair cut and styled just before her much-anticipated trip to Rome. She was very excited about her upcoming trip and began to describe it to Francoise, the owner of the salon, who was filling in for Ellen's regular stylist who, herself, was on vacation. Francoise was rather pretentious and considered himself a "man of the world" because he'd traveled a lot in his youth. He had opinions about everything, and wasn't afraid to share them.

True to form, Francoise said, "Rome! I've been there, and it's beyond me why anyone would want to vacation there. It's crowded, dirty, old, and full of Italians! But, that's your decision, I suppose. How do you plan to get there?"

Ellen enthusiastically told him about the deal she'd gotten through the airline she'd chosen. "We got a great rate, and I put it on their charge, earning a lot of extra frequent flyer miles. We even get to check our bags for free!"

"Oh, I hate that airline," Francoise exclaimed. "Their planes are old. Their flight attendants are ugly and surly. The food is bad. The seats are cramped, and they're always late. But I suppose you haven't much choice. Where are you staying in Rome?"

"Oh, we'll be at the Grand on the Via Veneto. Very highly recommended!" said Ellen.

"Say no more," said Francoise. "I know that place. Everyone thinks it's going to be something special, but it's just an American-owned dump. Really, the worst hotel in the city. The rooms are small; everything's old, and they're overpriced. Whatcha doing when you get there?"

By now, Ellen was starting to feel really disappointed about her vacation, but she was stuck there in the chair, so she replied, "Well, we're going to do the usual tourist stuff since we've never been there – you know, the Spanish Steps, the Colosseum, the Trevi Fountain, the Forum…and we're going to the Vatican! We hope to see the Pope!"

"The Pope!" Francoise snorted, "Good luck! You and a hundred thousand other people all will be trying to see him at the same time. Maybe you'll see him up on his balcony, waving down to the crowd. He'll look the size of an ant!"

A bit upset now, as she was leaving, Ellen tried to give Francoise a minimal tip, since he'd practically ruined the wonderful Roman holiday she'd been planning for so long.

"Well, good luck on that trip of yours," he said as she left. "You're going to need it."

A month later, Ellen returned, and her regular stylist was doing her hair. Before long, Francoise stopped by and asked her about Rome, prepared to give her a big "I told ya so!"

Instead, Ellen said, "It was wonderful! Not only were we on time in a brand new plane, but it was overbooked, and they bumped us up to first class. The food and wine were wonderful, and I had a handsome, young, Italian steward who waited on me hand and foot!

"And, Francoise, the hotel was great! They'd just finished a $5 million renovation and remodeling job, and now it's a jewel – the finest hotel in the city. They, too, were overbooked, so they apologized and gave us a huge executive suite at no extra charge!"

"Well!" said a deflated Francoise, "that's all well and good, but I know you didn't get to see the Pope!"

"Actually, we were quite lucky," said Ellen, "because as we toured the Vatican, a member of the Pope's staff – a Swiss Guard, I think it was – tapped me on the shoulder and explained that the Pope likes to meet some of his visitors. Amazingly enough, he asked us to step into the Pope's private anteroom and wait, and His Holiness would personally greet us. Sure enough, five minutes later, the Pope walked through the door and shook my hand! I knelt down, and he spoke a few words to me."

"Oh, really? What'd he say?" Francoise inquired, huffily.

He said, "Where'd you get the shitty hairdo?"

RAISIN BREAD

Becky was an extremely attractive, physically fit young lady, who was quite a fashionista. She worked as a clerk at the local bakery while attending college and spent a sizable portion of the paychecks she earned on the latest fashions. Becky particularly liked to wear short skirts and thong panties, which showed off her perfect legs to maximum advantage.

One day, a young man named Matt entered the store, glanced at Becky, and glanced at the shelves of bread behind the counter. Noticing the length of her skirt (or general lack thereof) and the location of the raisin bread, he had a brilliant idea. "I'd like some raisin bread please," Matt said politely. Becky nodded her head and climbed a ladder to reach the raisin bread, which happened to be located on the very top shelf. Matt, standing almost directly beneath her, was provided with an excellent view, just as he surmised he would.

Once Becky descended the ladder, Matt mumbled that he really should get two more loaves. Because he just remembered, he's having company over the weekend. As Becky climbed the ladder and retrieved the second and third loaves of bread, another male customer, Rick, walked in and noticed what was going on. Thinking quickly, Rick requested his own loaf of raisin bread, so he could continue to enjoy the view.

With each trip up the ladder, Becky seemed to catch the eye of another male customer. Pretty soon, every male patron was asking for raisin bread, just to see Becky, in her short skirt, climb up and down. After many trips, she was tired, irritated, and wondering why the raisin bread had suddenly become so popular!

Finally, once again at the top of the ladder, Becky turned and fumed, glaring at the men standing below. She noticed an elderly man standing among the crowd, staring up at her. Thinking to save herself a trip, Becky yelled down at the old man, "Is yours raisin too?"

"No," croaked the old man, "but it's startin' to twitch!"

BIRTHDAY WISH

Ed and Jackie had been married for 15 years. One evening, Ed was sitting on the edge of the bed, observing Jackie, who was across the room, standing in front of the mirror, brushing her hair. Since her birthday wasn't far off, he asked Jackie what she'd like to have for her birthday.

"Y'know, Ed, I'd really like to be six again," she replied, smiling.

That gave Ed a brilliant idea!

Saturday was Jackie's birthday, and Ed told her to set aside the whole day for a special birthday treat. That morning, Ed arose early, made Jackie a nice, big bowl of Lucky Charms, and happily took her to a huge theme park that was a short drive away. What a day! He put her on every ride in the park: the Death Slide, the Tower of Fear, the Wall of Terror, and the Screaming Monster Roller Coaster. He made sure he included "girlie" attractions, like the Carousel, the Ferris wheel, the Swirly Swing, the Tea Party Twirl, Strawberry Shortcake's Sleepover, and the My Little Pony Adventure. In between, Ed bought her treats like ice cream and cotton candy.

Five hours later, they staggered out of the theme park. Jackie's head was spinning, and she was on a major sugar buzz. But Ed wasn't finished. He took her to a McDonald's, where he ordered Jackie a Happy Meal and a chocolate shake. Then it was off to a movie, with popcorn, soda pop, and her favorite candy, M&Ms.

What a perfect, wonderful day! What a fabulous adventure! Finally, Ed and Jackie returned home and wobbled up the stairs, where Jackie collapsed into bed, exhausted, clutching the stuffed monkey Ed had won for her at the amusement park.

Ed walked over to the bed, leaned over his wife, and lovingly asked with a big smile, "Well dear, what was it like, being six again?"

Jackie's eyes slowly opened, and her expression suddenly

changed.

She said, "I meant my dress size, you dumb ass!"

LIFE IN THE HILLS

UBBA AND ELLIE led a quiet, sheltered life, in the remote wilderness of Appalachia. But, one day, Bubba decided it was about time to visit the city – although, in this case, the Big City was Critterville, a small town of a few hundred people.

Bubba ventured into the General Store, where he picked up a mirror and looked in it. Never having seen a mirror before, Bubba said, "Well, tarnation! Here's a picture of my pore, dead Pappy! Musta been took when he was just about as old as I am now!"

Bubba happily bought the mirror, but on the way home, he remembered that his wife, Ellie, never did take a likin' to his Pappy much at all! So, he hung the mirror in the back of the barn, where Ellie never went, and every morning, before leaving to work out in the fields, Bubba would sneak to the back of the barn and spend a few minutes just a-visitin' with his Pappy!

Ellie started getting suspicious when Bubba began leaving earlier every morning to do his chores and head out to the fields. So, she followed him one day, and saw that he was spending extra time in the barn. Immediately, Ellie wondered if Bubba might be a-messin' in the barn with that neighbor gal she'd heard about, who lived just across the ridge.

After Bubba left the barn one morning, she sneaked in and found the mirror. She looked into the glass and fumed, "So *this* is the ugly bitch he's been runnin' around with!"

Later, when Bubba and Ellie discovered what the mirror actually was, they patched things up in a big way: Ellie immediately became pregnant!

Nine months later, she went into labor in the middle of the night, and the doctor was called out from town to assist in the delivery. Since there was no electricity, the doctor handed Bubba a lantern and said, "Here, Bubba. You hold this here lantern high, so I can see what I'm doing when the baby comes out!"

Soon, a baby boy was brought into the world, and an excited Bubba began to lower the light and celebrate.

"Whoa there!" said the doctor. "Don't be in such a rush to put that lantern down, Bubba. I think there's another one a-comin'." And, sure enough, within minutes he had delivered a baby girl.

"Hold that lantern up! Don't set it down! There's another one!" said the doctor. And, within a few minutes, he had delivered a third baby.

"Wait!" cried the doctor yet again. "Don't put down that lantern yet! It looks to me like there's still *another* baby a-comin!"

At this point, a nervous and shaky Bubba scratched his head in bewilderment and said, "Doc, you reckon it might be the *light* that's attractin' 'em?"

AN IRISH LAD'S CONFESSION

TOMMY MORRISON, AN Irish lad in Limerick, went to confession. "Bless me, Father, for I have sinned," he began. "I have been with a loose woman."

The priest, Father Shanahan, asked, "Is that you, Tommy Morrison?"

"Yes, Father, it is," Tommy admitted.

"And who was the loose woman you were with?" asked Father Shanahan.

"Oh, sure an' I can't be tellin' ya that, Father," said Tommy. "I don't want to ruin her reputation."

"Well, Tommy," said the priest, "I'm sure to find out sooner or later, so ya may as well tell me now. Was it Brenda O'Malley?"

"I cannot say," said Tommy.

"Patricia Kelly?"

"I'll never tell."

"Bridget Shannon?" asked Father Shanahan.

"I'm sorry, but I can't name her, Father," said Tommy.

"Was it Cathy Morgan?"

"My lips are sealed."

Then it must have been Fiona McDonald," said Father Shanahan.

"Please. I cannot tell ya, Father," said Tommy.

"You're a steadfast lad, Tommy Morrison," said the priest. "I admire that, but you've sinned and you must atone. You cannot attend church for three months. Off with ya, now!"

Tommy walked back to his pew, where his friend, Sean, asked, "What'd ya get?"

And Tommy answered, "Three months' vacation and five good leads!"

SPEED TRAP

A YOUNG MAN with Michigan license plates was caught in a speed trap by the Mississippi State Police. A stereotypical southern police officer stepped out of his patrol car, adjusted his reflective sunglasses and Smokey the Bear hat, and swaggered up to the young man's window.

"Whu chew driving so fast fer, boy? You goin' to a fahhr? Lessee yore license, boy," said the cop.

As the young man was handing over his license, the officer looked in the back seat of the car, and noticed that it was full of large knives.

The officer said, "Tell me, boy, why you got them knives on that there back seat?"

The young man replied, "Well sir, I'm a juggler. I juggle knives in a night club act."

The officer spat some tobacco juice and said, "A juggler, eh? Well, don't that beat all! Then he said, "Awright, git outa the car, boy, an' put cha hands on the roof. You goin' to jail!"

The young man pleaded with the officer not to take him to jail. He offered to prove to the cop that he was a juggler by demonstrating his skill. He said, "You can even hold me at gunpoint while I juggle for you."

So, the officer reluctantly allowed the young guy to prove he could juggle knives while he held him at gunpoint.

Two miles down the road, at Boone's Tavern, Jim Bob was drinking with his buddy, R.J. Jim Bob soon left and got into his rusty, old pickup truck. He proceeded down the road, trying his best to stay on the right side of that there yaller line. It was then that Jim Bob spotted the most unbelievable sight of his life! He pulled over to the side of the road, dug his cell phone out of his jeans, punched-in the number for Boone's Tavern, and asked for his buddy, R.J.

When R.J. got on the phone, Jim Bob said, "Whatever you do when you leave that tavern, don't go north on Route 29. The po-lice are givin' a new sobriety test that *nobody* kin pass!"

THE OLD MAN AND THE KEYS

L ATE ONE AFTERNOON, a ragged old man shuffled into Kelly's Bar. Stinking of whiskey and cigarettes, he took the "Piano Player Wanted" sign from the window and, with shaking hands, gave it to Wally, the bartender.

"I'd like to apply for this here job," he said.

Wally wasn't too sure about the old guy. It looked like he'd already had a few drinks before he came in, and he wasn't all that presentable. But it had been awhile since Kelly's Bar had a piano player, and business was falling off. Wally figured if the guy was any good, he could clean him up and put him to work.

"Tell me about yourself," said Wally.

"Well, my name's Cap'n Jack," he said. "I was a ship's captain in the Merchant Marine. Sailed the oceans and the Great Lakes. Learned to play piano when I was a kid and kept it up over the years whenever I could find a piano to play. Even wrote a few tunes."

Still unsure about Cap'n Jack, Wally decided to give him a try. He really needed to attract more business. "Piano's over there," he said. "Let's hear what you can do."

The old sea captain staggered over to the piano and several bar patrons snickered. But by the time he was into the third bar of music, every voice in the saloon was silenced. What they heard was piano playing prowess unlike any of them had ever heard before, let alone in an old downtown bar. When the old sailor finished, they burst into applause. Some had tears in their eyes.

The bartender brought Cap'n Jack a beer and told him he sounded wonderful. "What do you call that tune?" he asked.

"It's called 'Drop Your Drawers, Baby, We're Gonna Rock Tonight," said Cap'n Jack. "Wrote it myself," he said as he took a long drink of beer. "I got others," he said.

The old sea captain began playing another tune, this one a knee-slapping, hand-clapping bit of ragtime that had the place jumping. People were starting to come in from the street to hear the old guy play. When he finished, the old seaman acknowledged the applause and told the crowd the tune was called, "Big Boobs Raise My Anchor". He then excused himself and lurched off to the men's room.

After thinking about it a bit, Wally decided to hire the guy, regardless of the weird and kinky names he had for his tunes, and no matter how unkempt he looked. Maybe he could just spruce up the guy's appearance and keep him from announcing the names of the pieces.

When the old sea captain came out of the men's room, the bartender went over to tell him he had the job, but noticed that the old man's fly was open and his penis was hanging out.

Wally said, "The job is yours, Cap'n Jack, but – before you rejoin the crowd out there –do you know your fly's open and your penis is hanging out?"

"Know it!?" said Cap'n Jack, "Hell, I *wrote* it!"

ORIGINAL EQUIPMENT

JESS WAS A young, athletic guy who loved to participate in sports. He played tennis and handball, was in an adult soccer league, was a scratch golfer, and even played shortstop on his company's baseball team.

Life was just great for Jess because he was about to be married to Kelly, the love of his life, who was not only knockout gorgeous but also a virgin – truly a rarity, these days.

A week before the wedding, Jess was batting in the 8th Inning of his team's baseball game and took a high-speed fastball right in the crotch. Like many of the guys in this amateur league, he wasn't wearing any protection and, writhing in agony, Jess fell to the ground. He was taken out of the game and, the next morning, he took himself to the doctor.

Jess said, "How bad is it, doc? I'm getting married next week, and my fiancé is still a virgin. I don't want this to wreck my honeymoon!"

The doctor said, "I think you'll be OK. I'll have to put your penis in a splint. However, to keep it straight and let it heal properly. It should be fine."

The doctor then took four tongue depressors, and formed a neat, little, 4-sided splint, then taped it all together – altogether, an impressive work of medical art!

Jess didn't mention any of this to Kelly. The following week, they were married in a gala ceremony and, immediately after a brief reception, went to a nearby resort to begin their honeymoon.

That night in the room, Kelly took off her blouse to reveal her beautiful breasts. She said, "You're the first, Jess! No other man has *ever* touched these!"

Jess immediately dropped his pants and said, "And look at *this*, Kelly! Still in the *crate!*"

WHAT ARE FRIENDS FOR?

F RED AND JOHN were the best of friends and long-time drinking buddies.

One night, both Fred and John were "over-served" even more than usual, and the three orders of buffalo wings with Fire-In-The-Hole Hot Sauce didn't help. In fact, the combination of wings and brewskis caused John to toss his cookies – or, in this case, the aforementioned chicken – all over the front of his sports coat.

"Holy Mother o' Hops!" said John. "My wife ish gonna kill me!"

Despite the barf down the front of John's blazer, Fred gave him a hug, put his arm around John's shoulder, and stuck $20 in the front pocket of his sport coat. He said, "Don' worry, John, ol' pal, ol' bud, ol'…pa-ud! I'm yer besht fren, ain' I? Huh? So you show her thish twenny in yer pocket, an' tell 'er ol' Freddie boy – thash me, remember? – up-chucked on yer jacket, an' that I gave you thish money to get it cleaned!"

John looked at Fred through crimson eyes and began to get a little misty. "Thash fan-tashtic, Fred ol' buddy! You'd do thish fer me? You're amaszhing! The besht! Really!"

John staggered home, and no sooner did he open the door than his wife Paula began shouting, "John! Where the hell have you been? Just look at you!"

As quickly as his wasted condition would allow, John replied, "Aw, look, Paula, dearisht! Ish not really my fault! Fred ate too many beefa-boofa-buffoo-chicken wings, an' thoo up all over me. But look," he added, grabbing the money out of his front jacket pocket and handing it over, "Fred's such a shweet guy, he gave me thish 20 bucks t'get my jacket cleaned!"

"But there are 40 dollars here!" Paula said.

"Oh, yeah, I forgot," said John, thinking quickly, his poor, besotted brain now having to work overtime. "Fred crapped in my pants, too!"

LIKE IT WAS YESTERDAY

AUDREY AND BOB were childhood sweethearts. They'd known each other all their lives. They grew up together, went to school together, married, settled down in the same neighborhood, and raised a wonderful family. Now, Audrey and Bob were celebrating their 60th wedding anniversary.

The old neighborhood was still safe and flourishing, and the Catholic school from which they'd both graduated was still thriving. The school was hosting an open house, encouraging students from throughout the area to enroll, and Audrey and Bob decided to visit.

They walked to their old school, hand-in-hand, as they did as teenagers. They went inside and looked around, letting pleasant memories wash over them. They even found an old desk they'd shared. Bob had carved "Bob + Audrey" into the underside of the desktop.

As they were walking home, hand-in-hand, an armored car rounded the corner, and a bag of money fell out, practically at their feet. Bob picked it up, but they didn't know what to do, because the vehicle didn't even slow down. So, they took the money home, and Audrey counted it. There was $50,000!

Bob said, "We've got to give it back."

Audrey said, "Finders keepers, Bob! The Good Lord wants us to have this money. He practically dropped it in our laps!" And she put the money back in the bag and hid it in the attic.

The next day, two federal agents stopped by. They were going door-to-door, asking residents if anyone knew about money that fell out of an armored car the day before.

Audrey said, "No, I don't know about any money."

Bob said, "She's lying. We found it, and she hid it up in the attic."

Audrey said, "Don't believe him. He's getting senile."

The agent said, "Sir, why don't you tell us the story from the beginning?"

Bob said, "Well, yesterday, when Audrey and I were walking home from school..."

The agent looked at his partner and said, "C'mon, Ray, we're outta here!"

THE THREE BARS

THREE FRIENDS, SEAN, Angelo, and Chet, were in a bar, having a terrific time, drinking, telling tall tales and, in general, shooting the breeze. They all agreed that the tavern they were in was a pretty nice place. But, after giving it some thought – not to mention a snootful of drinks – each of them said he knew of a better place.

Sean said, "Aye, I know of a great bar down on the South Side named O'Brien's. At O'Brien's, after you buy two drinks, O'Brien himself – bein' a fine broth of a lad and a genuine Son of the Old Sod – will pay for your third drink!"

Angelo and Chet agreed that O'Brien's sounded like quite a nice place, but Angelo knew of a better one.

He said, "Over in Little Italy, dere's a bar called Vinnie's Tavern. At Vinnie's, you buy a drink, Vinnie buys you a drink. You buy anudda drink, and Vinnie buys you anudda drink."

The three friends all agreed that Vinnie's Tavern sounded even better than O'Brien's, but then Chet piped up. He said, "You tink *dat's* great? I'll show ya great! In my old neighborhood, dere's dis place called Turkowski's. At Turkowski's, dey buy you your first drink. Den dey buy you your second drink. Den dey buy you your tird drink. And *den* dey take you in da back and get you laid!"

"Mamma mia!" said Angelo.

"Faith an' begorrah!" said Sean. Then, they paused and thought awhile – as well as they could, given the condition they were in – and Sean said to Chet, "That's kind of unbelievable." And Angelo said, "Did dat actually happen to you, Chet?"

And Chet said, "No, but it happened to my sister!"

JESUS IS WATCHING!

A BURGLAR BROKE into a suburban house one night when he was sure that the owners were away. He shone his flashlight around the family room, looking for easily portable valuables. Spotting an iPad, he picked it up and started to put it in his sack.

Suddenly, he heard a strange, disembodied voice coming out of the dark, saying, "Jesus is watching you!"

The burglar nearly jumped out of his skin. A chill ran up his spine. His hair stood on end, and he quickly extinguished the flashlight and froze. When he heard nothing more after awhile, he shook his head to clear it, promised himself a nice vacation after his next big score, turned on the light, and continued his search for more valuables.

He had just put an iPod into his sack and was headed for the bedroom where the jewelry, no doubt, awaited him when he again heard the spooky voice say, "Jesus is watching you!"

The burglar freaked out now and frantically swept the room with his light. Finally, in the corner of the room, his flashlight beam shakily came to rest on a parrot.

"Did you say that?" he hissed at the parrot.

"Awk! I said it! I said it!," the parrot announced. Then he squawked, "Just trying to warn you! Trying to warn you!"

The burglar relaxed, now that he saw his adversary was nothing more than a talking bag of feathers. "Warn me, huh? And just who the heck do you think you are, warning me?" he said.

"Awk! I'm Moses!" said the parrot.

"Moses!?" the burglar sneered. "What kind of people would name a parrot *Moses?*"

The bird promptly answered, "Awk! The same people who named their 140-pound Rottweiler *Jesus!*"

HAUL PASS

K EVIN WAS A strong, good-looking, muscular guy who worked on a farm. One Saturday morning, he jumped on his motorcycle and headed for town to pick up a few odds and ends.

Just outside of town, Kevin's bike broke down, and he took it to the shop in town to have it repaired. They couldn't do it while he waited, so Kevin said, "Well, I don't live that far. I'll just pick up the things I came to town for, carry them back to the farm, and come back for the bike this afternoon before you close."

Kevin then went to the hardware store, and bought a big, strong, galvanized bucket, and a small anvil. He then stopped by the market, and picked up a couple of chickens and a live goose. Now, however, Kevin had a problem: how was he going to carry all of his purchases home?

The feed store owner said, "Why don't you put the anvil in the bucket, carry the bucket in one hand, put a chicken under each arm, and carry the goose in your other hand?"

"Hey, great idea!" said Kevin, and out the door he went.

In the parking lot, he was stopped by a little old lady who was lost. "Can you tell me how to get to 163 Elm Street?" she asked.

Kevin said, "Well, I live on a farm at the end of Elm Street, and I know a shortcut down this alley. Why don't you just walk with me, and we'll be there in no time!"

The little old lady looked at the handsome bodybuilder suspiciously. She said, "I'm a lonely widow without a husband to defend me. How do I know that you won't get me in that alley, hold me against the wall, pull up my skirt, and have your way with me?"

Kevin was astonished. "Holy smokes, lady! I'm carrying a bucket, an anvil, two chickens and a live goose. How in the world could I possibly hold you up against the wall and do that?"

The little old lady said, "Set the goose down, cover him with the bucket, put the anvil on top of the bucket, and I'll hold the chickens!"

THE WAGER

A WEALTHY TEXAN was vacationing in Ireland. One evening, he and his entourage walked into a pub in the hardscrabble town of Limerick and announced, "I hear you Irish are a bunch of hard drinkers. I'll give 500 American dollars to anyone in here who can drink 10 pints of Guinness in a row tonight."

The pub became very quiet. No one took up the Texan on his offer. One man – O'Leary – even walked out the back door.

A half-hour later, O'Leary returned and asked the Texan, "Is your wager still good?"

The Texan said, "Why, it shore is! 500 American dollars if y'all can drink 10 pints in a row!" Then, he reached in his jacket, pulled out his billfold, removed $500, and set it down on the bar.

The pub owner lined up 10 pints of Guinness on the bar, and O'Leary began to drink. The other pub patrons cheered him as he drank, pint after pint. The Texan stared in amazement. Unbelievably, O'Leary managed to down all 10 pints of Guinness without stopping! He slapped down the last empty glass on the bar with a flourish, wiped his mouth with his sleeve, and smiled as the crowd cheered and the Texan took the $500 and handed it to him.

The Texan said, "Well, if that don't beat all! Congratulations! But, if ya don't mind me askin', where did y'all go for that 30 minutes when you left the pub after I announced the wager?"

O'Leary quietly burped and answered, "Well sir, before I took ya up on yer wager, I just had to go to the pub down the street to see if I could do it!"

Happy Endings

BLUE BLOOD VS. BLUE COLLAR

THREE COLLEGE KIDS from wealthy families and Ivy League schools were traveling by train along with three kids who attended a state university and came from blue collar families. They were all headed to a bowl game in Florida.

At the train station, the three rich guys each bought a ticket and watched as the three not-so-rich guys bought just one ticket. "How are the three of you going to travel on only one ticket?" asked Todd, one of the wealthy guys.

"Watch and learn," said Brian, one of the blue collar kids.

All six students boarded the train. The three wealthy guys took their respective seats, but the three blue collar boys crammed together in one of the train's rest rooms and closed the door.

Shortly after the train got underway, the conductor came around, collecting tickets. He knocked on the lavatory door and said, "Ticket, please!" The door opened a crack, and a single arm emerged, holding a ticket. The conductor took it and moved on, and the three guys emerged from the toilet and took their seats.

The three Ivy Leaguers saw this scenario unfold and agreed that it was pretty clever. So, the day after the game, they got together with the three State College boys and told them they'd like to do the same thing, just for kicks, on the return trip.

When they got to the station, the Ivy Leaguers bought a single ticket for the return trip. But, much to their astonishment, they saw that the State College guys didn't buy any ticket at all!

"How are you going to travel without a ticket?" said Troy, one of the rich kids.

"Watch and learn," said Mike, one of the blue collar boys.

When they boarded the train, the three wealthy kids hid in a rest room, and the three blue collar kids crammed into another rest room. As soon as the train got underway, Mike left the blue-collar kids' lavatory and walked over to the toilet in which the wealthy kids were hiding.

He knocked on the door and said, "Ticket, please!"

TOUGH GUY

RYAN WALKED INTO a tavern he'd never been to before in a rough neighborhood. He immediately spotted a huge jar on the back bar behind the muscular bartender. It was filled with $20 bills. There must have been thousands of dollars in that enormous jar!

Naturally, Ryan asked the barkeep, "What's up with the jar?"

The bartender paused from wiping a glass, and said, "Well, we call it the Tough Guy Jar. You put $20 in the jar, and if you pass three tough tests, you get all the money in the jar. A lot of men have tried. A lot of men have failed."

Ryan wasn't one to pass up an opportunity to win thousands of bucks. He asked, "What are the three tests?"

"Uh-uh," said the bartender. "First you pay – then I tell you what the three tests are. They're tough – no one has ever passed them – and they're weird, but they're all do-able."

So, Ryan gave the bartender $20. He stuffed it into the jar and said, "Here's what you gotta do: First, you gotta drink a whole half-gallon of this hot pepper tequila we've got here, including the worm at the bottom, all at once – preferably without making wussy faces, screaming, or carrying on. Second, there's a pit bull chained up out in back, with a sore tooth. You gotta yank out his sore tooth with your *bare hands!* And third, there's an old woman upstairs who's never had an orgasm during sex. You have to make things right and satisfy her."

"Are you insane?" said Ryan. "First of all, you'd have to be nuts to drink a half-gallon of hot pepper tequila! And those other things are not only weird, but they sound *horrible!*"

"Suit yourself," said the barkeep, "but your 20 bucks stays in the jar."

Ryan decided to stick around and have a few drinks, despite foolishly giving the bartender $20 before hearing the three Tough Guy tests. And, while stewing over his stupidity, he began to get pretty stewed himself. He kept looking at the huge jar filled with cash. After a few drinks, the jar began looking bigger and the fortune began looking more and more massive!

After several more drinks, Ryan was totally blasted. Finally, he called the bartender over and said, "Barr-thendererrrr! Wh-wh-wherrre'zaaaat teq-teq-tequiiiillllaaa?"

The bartender hauled out the half-gallon jug of fiery hot, red pepper tequila. Ryan grabbed it with both hands and resolutely chugged it down. Tears were streaming down his face. His head was covered with sweat, and some of the concoction had spilled down his chin and shirt-front, but he managed to finish it without screaming, choking, panting for air, or making a face! And, now he was about as intoxicated as you can get without passing out.

Barely able to walk, Ryan staggered out back, to where the pit bull was chained up.

Everyone in the bar heard the furious commotion out in the alley. They heard a huge, noisy, knock-'em-down-drag-'em-out fight. They heard the pit bull growling and barking. They heard Ryan screaming and swearing. They heard crashing and smashing sounds. They imagined a horrible, bloody scene unfolding, as Ryan somehow removed the big dog's tooth. Suddenly, they heard the pit bull yelp – then, silence. They figured Ryan surely must be dead. No one wanted to go out and look.

A few minutes passed, and the back door swung open and hit the wall with a bang. There stood Ryan, drenched with sweat, his face beet red, his shirt shredded, his pants torn, one shoe missing, and terrible, bloody scratches all over his body. He stood just inside the door, panting and trying to catch his breath. Then, he staggered forward a few steps and, grabbing the edge of the bar to hold himself upright, said:

"Nowww, where'sh that ol' wommannn with the sore tooth?"

FITTING PUNISHMENT

L IFE IS DIFFERENT, down on the farm. Life's lessons are taught in more direct, pragmatic ways, and are, thus, more memorable.

One day, young Johnny was working on his family's farm, and things just weren't going his way. He awoke particularly hungry and grumpy that morning, but when he went downstairs for breakfast, his mother insisted, "No breakfast 'til you do your morning chores."

This upset him even more, and his growling stomach didn't improve his mood. After milking the cow, Johnny angrily slapped her rump and kicked over the milking stool. On his way to the chicken coop to gather eggs, he gave the rooster a kick, and made loud noises to scare the hens. Johnny even gave the old sow's ear a yank, as part of his temper tantrum. Starving, he returned to the house.

Johnny's mother, who had been watching his antics from the window, said, "I saw you slap old Marybelle and, just for that, you'll be getting no milk for breakfast. Also, for kicking the rooster and scaring the chickens, you'll get no eggs today. And, for mistreating the poor pig like that, you'll get no bacon, either!"

The young boy sat in his chair and sulked, left with just some dry biscuits for breakfast.

Just then, Johnny's father came in through the back door. He was also in an ugly mood. As he entered the house, he nearly fell over the family cat. He angrily booted it out of the way, and the cat ran, yowling, out of the house.

Johnny watched all of this carefully, then looked at his angry mother, then back at his Dad, and said, "Uh, oh, Dad! You know what THAT means!"

HAM SANDWICH

A PRIEST AND a rabbi were traveling together on a plane. After awhile, the priest turned to the rabbi and asked, "Excuse me, rabbi, but I was wondering: is it still a requirement of your faith that you refrain from eating pork?"

The rabbi responded, "Yes, that is still one of our beliefs."

The priest then asked, "Have you ever eaten pork?"

The rabbi said, "Well, yes, on one occasion, many years ago, I did succumb to temptation and tasted a ham sandwich."

The priest nodded in understanding and resumed reading his book.

A short time later, the rabbi turned to the priest and asked him, "Father, is it still a requirement of the Catholic Church that you remain celibate?"

The priest nodded, and said, "Yes, rabbi, that is still very much a part of our faith."

The rabbi then asked him, "Father, have you ever given in to the temptation of the flesh?"

The priest blushed and said, "Yes, rabbi, on one occasion, several years ago, I was weak and broke with my faith."

The rabbi nodded understandingly and went back to his reading. He was silent for about five minutes and then he said, "Beats a ham sandwich, doesn't it?"

THE PUZZLE

MINDY WAS AN attractive young woman who, unfortunately, happened to be blonde. As a result, she was always chided for doing stereotypically "blonde" things – or not being the brightest bulb on the Christmas tree, so to speak.

One evening, Mindy was working on a jigsaw puzzle that she just couldn't figure out. Apparently, it was one of those with 1,000 small pieces that are so difficult to assemble. After awhile, in frustration, Mindy phoned her boyfriend Karl, and said, "It's the hardest jigsaw puzzle I've ever seen. I just can't get any of the pieces to fit together."

Karl said, "Usually, I just look at the picture on the box. At the very least, the box cover shows you what the finished puzzle will look like. What is the finished puzzle supposed to be a picture of?"

Mindy said, "It's a picture of a tiger."

Well, Karl figured that didn't sound too difficult, so he said, "I'll be right over."

Karl went over to Mindy's house, and saw that Mindy had all of the puzzle pieces laid out on a card table. He looked at the picture on the box and studied the pieces on the table.

Mindy said, "Well, Karl, what do you think?"

And Karl said, "Mindy, I'm sorry to say that no matter how long you work on this puzzle, you'll never get these pieces to fit together. So, let's just relax, have a cup of coffee…and put the Frosted Flakes back in the box."

MAFIA BOOKKEEPER

I T'S A TOUGH job, but somebody's gotta do it: Bookkeeper for the Mafia Godfather.

Leo was originally chosen for the job, not only because he had an uncanny mind for math and accounting, but also because he was deaf and dumb. The Godfather figured a guy who could neither speak nor hear would be the ideal bookkeeper: He'd never hear anything he could testify about in court!

But, one day, the Godfather noticed that his account was missing 10 Million bucks – not a small chunk of change – and he strongly suspected Leo of stealing the money from him. You don't do this sort of thing to the mob, particularly to its leader.

When the Godfather went to shake down Leo for the money he embezzled, he took along his attorney Deano, who, having worked with the bookkeeper over the years, knew sign language, and could facilitate the conversation.

The Godfather asked the bookkeeper, "Where's the $10 Million you stole from me?"

The attorney, using sign language, asked Leo where the $10 Million was hidden.

The bookkeeper signed back: "I don't know what you're talking about."

Deano told the Godfather, "He says he doesn't know what you're talking about."

The Godfather pulled out a .38 revolver, put it to Leo's temple, cocked it, and said, "Ask him again! Where's my money?"

The attorney signed to the bookkeeper: "He'll kill you for sure if you don't tell him."

Leo signed back: "OK! You win! I give up! The $10 Million is in a tool box, buried behind the shed in my cousin Enzio's backyard in Queens!"

The Godfather asked Deano, "What did he say?"

And the attorney replied, "He says you ain't got the guts to pull the trigger!"

ALL ABOARD!

JOHN WAS TRAVELING by train and estimated that he was getting close to his destination. So, he asked the conductor, "What time does the train stop in Farmington?"

"I'm sorry, sir," said the conductor, "but this train doesn't stop in Farmington."

"Doesn't stop in Farmington!?" John shouted. "But I've *gotta* get off in Farmington! I've got a meeting there in a half-hour, and I just *can't* miss it!"

"Well, look," said the conductor, "there may be one thing we can do, although we've never tried it before. Biff, the porter here, is a bodybuilder, and can lift a lot of weight. The station platform at Farmington is extra long. So, I'm thinkin' that Biff can dangle you out the door here, near the front of the train, and you move your legs as fast as you can, like you're running. We'll have the engineer slow down as much as he can – to about 25 miles an hour – and you keep pumping your arms and legs as fast as you can, and Biff will lower you onto the platform. Once you're on the platform and actually running, you can slow yourself down."

"Well, it's worth a try," said John. "I've *gotta* be in Farmington in a half-hour!

As they approached the Farmington platform, the train slowed down to 40, 30, then 25 MPH. Biff dangled John in mid-air out the door, and John started running in mid-air. Then, Biff lowered John down, and John made contact with the platform. His shoes started smoking; his heel snapped off; he heard things rip and tear, but – miracle of miracles – it worked! He was actually running down the platform at 25 miles an hour! Other passengers stared in amazement!

But then, as the caboose went by, a beefy hand attached to a muscular arm grabbed John by the shirt collar, lifted him up, and pulled him right back onto the train!

When John stood up, he saw Jed – an even *more* muscular, *more* powerful train porter than Biff! And, as he dusted John off, Jed happily said, "Man, y'all are lucky I seen you runnin' to catch yore train and grabbed ya! This here train don't even STOP in Farmington!

EFFICIENCY

TODAY, IT SEEMS, there are consultants for everything. Consultants, particularly time efficiency experts, often can make a noticeable difference in the way a business is run and the way it is perceived.

An example of how efficiency experts can affect a business is my recent visit to an upscale restaurant in town, where each of the waiters carried a spoon in his shirt pocket. It seemed a little strange, so when our waiter served our soup, I asked him, "Why does each of the waiters carry a spoon in his shirt pocket?"

"Well," he explained, "The restaurant's owners just hired Johnson Consulting to review our efficiency and revamp our processes, and after several months of analysis, they concluded that the spoon is the most frequently dropped utensil at a restaurant. About three spoons per hour are dropped by customers every day. By carrying a spoon in our pocket, we waiters can immediately replace a customer's dropped spoon, and drastically reduce the number of trips we'd have to make back to the kitchen.

As luck would have it, I dropped my spoon while he was talking, and he replaced it immediately. He then said, "See? I can get another spoon the next time I go to the kitchen, rather than make a special trip right now."

I was impressed.

Later, I also noticed a black string hanging out of the fly in our waiter's black trousers. Looking around, I noticed that each of the waiters – all of whom were male – had a similar, almost invisible, string hanging from their flies, as well. So, the next time our waiter came to the table, I gestured toward the front of his pants, and asked him, "Excuse me, but could you tell me why each of the waiters has a string right there? Is that also an efficiency thing?"

"Oh, why yes, sir, it is!" the waiter said, a bit self-consciously. Then he lowered his voice and said, "Not everyone is so observant as you, but the consulting firm I told you about also discovered that we can save time in the rest room. By tying this string to our you-know-what, we can pull it out without touching it, and eliminate the need to spend the extra time necessary to wash our hands. The consultants estimate this shortens our time spent in the rest room 76%.

"Hmmnn," I said, "but after you get it out, how do you put it back?"

"Well," he whispered, "I don't know about the other waiters, but I use the spoon."

HIS FINAL HOURS

LATE ONE MORNING, on his way home from a doctor's exam, Steve stopped in at his wife Judy's office to give her the bad news: the doctor said his condition had worsened. In fact, unbelievably, Steve had only 20 hours to live.

Wiping away Judy's tears, Steve asked her to make love to him. Of course, she agreed and, ignoring her current heavy workload, they locked Judy's office door and spent the lunch hour eagerly making love, right on her office couch.

Five hours later, at home, Steve approached Judy again and said, "Sweetheart, now I have only 13 hours or so left to live. Do you think we could make love again?" Judy, of course, consented, and they again made passionate love.

That night, as they were getting into bed, Steve realized that he now had roughly eight hours left to live. He touched Judy's shoulder, and said, "Honey? Please? This is our last night together. Can we make love just one more time before I die?"

Well, Judy simply couldn't resist Steve's heartfelt final request, and they made love once again. She then kissed Steve, rolled over, and went to sleep. Meanwhile, Steve stared at the ceiling, unable to sleep, the clock ticking in his head. Dead by morning. How could that be? Where did all the years go?

He tossed and turned until he was down to only four hours to live. And, even though it was the middle of the night, he tapped his wife on the shoulder to awaken her. "Judy, dear?" he sobbed, "I have only four hours left. Could we? Would you?"

Judy suddenly bolted up in bed, turned to him, and said, "Listen, Steve, I have to get up in the morning. You don't!"

GHOST CAR

IT WAS A dark and stormy night in Louisiana bayou country. Leroy was hitchhiking along a narrow, two-lane road in a monsoon-like rainstorm, trying to get to town. Actually, anyplace dry, with electricity and a roof, would be welcome.

Time passed slowly. The wind howled and visibility was so poor, Leroy could barely see his hand at the end of his arm. Still, he trudged on. Then, suddenly, something made him turn around and look back down the road behind him. What he saw gave him goose bumps. It was a pair of yellowed headlights, on a vehicle approaching slowly and silently, ghostlike in the rain. The car slowly crept toward him and stopped next to the hitchhiking Leroy.

Soaked through to the skin and desperate for a ride, Leroy gratefully jumped inside the car and slammed the door, and the car began moving again. Leroy turned toward the driver to thank him for stopping, but there was no one behind the wheel! In fact, the driver's side window was wide open, and gusts of wind lashed the vinyl driver's seat with rain.

Now, the car was picking up speed, and through the mist and raindrops on the windshield, Leroy saw that they were approaching a curve. He prepared to open the passenger's door and dive out as the curve came closer and closer, but he was too frightened. Then, out of the corner of his eye, he saw a ghostly, disembodied, gloved hand grip the steering wheel and guide the vehicle around the bend. Now, paralyzed with fear, Leroy just squeezed his eyes shut as the car continued slowly down the road in the thunderstorm.

Finally, Leroy'd had all he could take. He was scared to death and, as the car rolled through another curve, he jumped from the vehicle, rolled like he saw stuntmen do in the movies, came up on his feet, and took off, running down the road.

Leroy soon came to town. Wet and in shock, he burst into a bar that was, mercifully, open. With a quivering voice, he ordered a shot of bourbon and a beer.

"What in tarnation happened to you?" asked the bartender, looking at the trembling Leroy. And Leroy launched into a detailed description of his supernatural experience. The bartender and the other patrons got goose bumps as Leroy recounted his terrifying tale. He told it with such detail that they immediately knew he was telling the truth and wasn't just some drunken stranger. A hush fell over the tavern.

A half-hour later, the silence was broken and the tavern patrons jumped almost in unison when the door suddenly slammed open and two huge men stepped in. Both of the men were dressed in long slickers and drenched from head to toe. Perhaps they'd seen the ghost car too!

The two men walked up to the bar, and looked over to where Leroy was standing, still shaking. Then, one of the men spoke. In a deep voice with a Louisiana accent, he said to his companion, "Look, Boudreaux! Dere's dat idiot who rode in our car when we was pushin' it down da road in da rain!"

SEX AFTER DEATH?

Bob and Denise enjoyed married life. Especially the sex part. Their two biggest loves were sex and playing golf. In fact, Bob and Denise even lived right on a golf course, so they could play as often as possible.

Bob and Denise were married for many years, and as they got into their senior years, they decided to make a pact: Whoever died first would somehow come back and inform the other if there was sex after death. Their biggest fear was that there was no afterlife at all.

Bob was the first to die. And, true to his word, he contacted Denise as soon as he could.

"Denise...Denise..." Bob said.

"Is that you, Bob?" she said.

"Yes, dear, I've come back, like we agreed," he said.

"That's wonderful, sweetheart! What's it like?" she said.

"Well," he said, "I get up in the morning and have sex. Then I have breakfast, and then it's off to the golf course. I have sex again, bathe in the warm sun, then have sex a couple of more times."

"Oh, my!" said Denise.

"Next, I have lunch," Bob continued. "You'd be proud of my diet here, Denise – lots of greens. Then, after another tour around the golf course, I pretty much spend the rest of the afternoon having sex. After supper, it's back to the golf course, and more sex until late at night. Then, I catch up on some much-needed sleep, and the next day, it starts all over again."

"Oh, Bob, are you in heaven?" said Denise.

"No," he said, "I'm a rabbit in Arizona."

ONE SMART DOG

CHESTER AND EARL worked together as mechanics. They decided that a nice vacation would be to rent a cabin up north for a week and do some fishing and hunting. They took along Chester's dog, Barney, who was supposed to be a very good duck hunting dog.

The first morning at the cabin, Chester said to Earl, "Before we walk all the way to the duck pond, let me just send Barney ahead of us, to see if there are any ducks out there today. If there ain't, there's no use of us goin' to the pond this morning.

Chester sent his dog out to the pond. The dog came back and barked twice.

Chester said, "Well, I ain't goin' out right now. He only saw two ducks out there."

Earl said, "What? You're gonna take the dog's barks for truth? I don't believe it!" And, with that, Earl walked down to the duck pond to look for himself.

When Earl came back, he said to Chester, "Holy cow, man! That dog was right! There's only two ducks out there! Where did you get that dog?"

Chester said, "Well, I got him from a breeder just up the road. If you want, we can go see him and get a dog for you, too."

So, Earl went to see the breeder and asked for a dog like Barney, who can count ducks. The breeder sold Earl a dog named Buster.

The next morning, Earl sent Buster out to see how many ducks are on the pond. A few minutes later, Buster came back with a stick in his mouth, and started to hump Earl's leg. Outraged, Earl took the dog back to the breeder and said, "I want my money back! This dog's a fraud! I sent him to count how many ducks were on the pond, and all he did was come back with a stick in his mouth and start humping my leg!"

The breeder said, "There's nothin' wrong with this dog, Earl. He was just trying to tell you there are more f--king ducks out there than you can shake a stick at!"

ANOTHER SMART DOG

MARTY WAS DRIVING through the Texas panhandle one day when he saw a sign in front of a house: *TALKING DOG FOR SALE.* Marty pulled into the driveway, walked up to the house, rang the bell, and inquired about the dog.

"He's right out back," said the owner. "C'mon back, and I'll show him to y'all."

Marty walked to the back yard with the owner and saw a black Lab sitting there.

Marty walked up to the dog and said, "You talk?"

To Marty's total amazement, the dog replied, "Yep."

Marty checked to see if it was some sort of ventriloquist trick on the part of the owner, who was busy drinking a glass of iced tea when the dog was speaking.

"So, what's your story?" Marty said to the dog.

The Lab looked up and said, "Well, I discovered this gift of mine when I was pretty young, and I wanted to help the government, so I showed the CIA I could talk, and they immediately had me jetting from country to country, sitting in rooms with spies and world leaders, listening, and reporting on them. No one suspected a dog would be eavesdropping. I was one of their most valuable operatives until I got tired of all the travel. So, I signed up for a job at an airport here in Texas, and worked airport security for awhile. I was able to listen in on a lot of suspicious characters and uncover some pretty incredible dealings. I was awarded a batch of medals, then settled down, sired a few litters of puppies, and now I'm just retired."

"That's amazing," Marty said and asked the owner, "How much do you want for him?"

The owner said, "20 bucks should do it."

Marty was astounded, "This dog is amazing! Why do you want to sell him for just 20 dollars?"

The owner replied, "He's a liar. He didn't do any of that stuff!"

ITALIAN HONEYMOON

Y EARS AGO, BEFORE air travel became more practical and economical, most people traveled long distances by train. And so it was that, in 1950, a humble New York barber, an Italian immigrant named Mario, took his new bride, named Virginia, to Florida for their honeymoon. For many years, South Florida had been a popular spot for honeymoons and vacations for New Yorkers.

When he returned from his honeymoon, the guys at the barbershop pressed Mario for all of the juicy details of his trip – within the boundaries of good taste, of course.

Mario's friend, Giovanni, led off: "Hey, Mario! How was-a da treep?"

Mario said, "Everyt'ing was-a perfecto, except for dat damn train-a ride down."

"Whadda you mean?" said his buddy, Luigi.

"Well, we boarda da train atta Gran' Central Station. My beautiful Virginia, she packa da big-a basket food, wit-a san'wiches, cheese, vino, nice-a cigar for me, everyt'ing you could-a tink of. Everyt'ing is okey-doke 'til we get-a hungry and open-a lunch basket. Da conductore, he come-a by, wagga his finger, an' say, 'No eat in-a dis car. Must use-a da Dining Car!'

"OK, so me an' my wonderful Virginia, we go to-a da Dining Car and eat our big-a pic-a-nic lunch. Den we start to open-a vino, when da conductore he come by, wagga his finger, an' say, 'No drink in-a dis car. You must use-a Club Car!' Another rule to-a follow!

"OK, so I go with-a lovely Virginia to-a Club Car and drink-a de vino. Den I start to light-a my big cigar, and da conductore come again! Dis time he wagga da finger an' say, 'No smoke in-a dis car. Must go to Smokin-a Car.' So we go to Smokin-a Car, and I enjoy-a cigar.

"By now, it's-a late, so my beautiful Virginia and I go to da

Sleeper Car and-a go to bed. It's our honeymoon, eh? So we just about to start a boomada-boomada in da bed, an' dat damn conductore, he come-a down-a da hall, shouting atta top o' his-a voice, 'Nofolka Virginia! Nofolka Virginia!'

"Dat's-a da last-a time I'm-a take-a da damn train! We came-a home onna bus!"

THE BAR BET

A HANDSOME, RUGGED-LOOKING guy walked into a bar with a large pit bull by his side. Discretion being the better part of valor, the bartender chose not to ask the guy to take his dog and leave.

So, the big guy set the dog down on a stool and took the stool next to him. He (the guy, not the dog) turned to the other bar patrons and announced, "I'll make y'all a deal. I'm going to open this dog's mouth and place my genitals inside – right between those razor-sharp teeth of his. The dog will keep his mouth shut for one full minute. He will then open his mouth, at which time I will remove my genitals, unscathed. In return for witnessing this amazing spectacle, each of you will buy me a drink!"

The crowd murmured their approval, so the man stood up, dropped his jeans, and placed his privates between the pit bull's jaws. The crowd gasped in unison, as the dog closed its mouth. After a minute, the guy grabbed a beer bottle and rapped the pit bull, hard, on the top of his head. This signaled the dog to open its mouth, and the man removed his genitals, unscathed, as promised.

The crowd cheered, and the first of several free drinks was delivered to the handsome stranger, in recognition of his brave and remarkable feat.

The man then announced, "I'll pay $100 to anyone who is willing to give it a try!"

A hush fell over the crowd. After awhile, a hand went up in the back of the bar, and a young, blonde woman timidly spoke up.

"I'll try," she said, "but you'll have to promise not to hit me on the head with a beer bottle!"

THE CABBIE AND THE NUN

IT WAS A blustery autumn night, and a cab driver picked up a nun who was signaling for a ride. The driver watched her as she climbed into the cab, and continued to stare at her in the rear-view mirror after she was seated. Finally, she asked him why he was staring.

"I have a question to ask you," the driver replied, "but I don't want to offend you."

She said, "My dear son, I'm sure you won't offend me. At my age, and living in this city, I've been around long enough to see and hear just about everything despite wearing this habit. I'm sure there is nothing you could ask me that I would find offensive."

"OK, then, here goes," said the cab driver. "Ever since I was a little boy, I've always wondered what it would be like to be kissed by a nun."

The nun responded, "Well, let's see what we can do about that. But first, you have to be single, and secondly, you must be Catholic."

Now, the cab driver was excited. He said, "Yes, sister, I am single, and yes, I'm Catholic, too!"

"OK," said the nun, "pull over into that side street there."

The driver pulled over, and the nun proceeded to give him a kiss that would make a hooker blush. But, when they got back on the road, the cab driver began crying.

"My dear child," said the nun, "why are you crying?"

"Forgive me, sister, but I've just done a terrible thing," said the driver. "I lied to you. I'm not single; I'm a married man. And I'm not even Catholic; I'm Jewish."

"Oh, that's OK," the nun said, "actually, my name is Fred, and I'm on my way to a Halloween party!"

THE ITALIAN FIREFIGHTERS

THERE WAS A sausage factory in a small town in New Jersey that, among other varieties of sausage, made some excellent pepperoni. They not only had a tried-and-true secret recipe that they'd perfected over the years, but also an exclusive drying process that made their pepperoni some of the finest available anywhere.

Late one night, a fire broke out inside the sausage factory, and soon the building was engulfed in flames. The alarm went out to all of the fire departments for miles around, many of which were volunteer departments in their rural communities.

When the first firefighters arrived, the sausage company president rushed to the fire chief and said, "All of our secret recipes, and the secret to our exclusive pepperoni drying process, are in a vault in the center of the plant. They have to be saved, or we're permanently out of business. So, I will donate $100,000 to the fire department that saves them." This offer was broadcast to all of the responding volunteer fire departments.

Suddenly, from down the road, a lone, weak siren could be heard, and another fire truck came into sight. It was the 1950s vintage truck belonging to a nearby group of volunteer firefighters who were all retired from city departments. Their average age was well over 65, and most of them were first generation Italian immigrants. No one really took them seriously.

But, to everyone's amazement, the little run-down fire engine, driven by the Italian immigrants, drove right past the other fire trucks without a moment's hesitation. They continued right smack into the center of the inferno that now engulfed the entire building. Outside, the other firefighters watched in amazement as the Italian old-timers, now in the middle of the blaze, jumped off their truck and fought to put out the fire and save the one-of-a-kind recipes as if they were fighting to save their own lives – which, indeed, they may have been.

Within a short time, the brave, old Italian firefighters had astonishingly managed to extinguish the fire, working from within the center of the plant and save the secret recipes.

The grateful sausage company president joyfully announced that the little brigade of firefighters had fought so valiantly and with such superhuman effort that he was raising their reward from $100,000 to $200,000. He walked over to the brave, elderly Italian firefighters, and personally thanked each one.

A TV news crew rushed in to capture the happy proceedings for that evening's newscast. The street reporter walked up to the little old Italian fire chief and said, "Chief, your crew is to be commended on their bravery, jumping right into the middle of that fire to put it out. What are you going to do with all that money?"

"Well, I'm-a tell you," said Chief Pasquale De Luccinellavanti, the 70-year-old fire chief, "da first-a ting we-a gonna do is fix-a de brakes on-a dat sominabeech trock!"

A TOUCHING LOVE STORY

O N THEIR WEDDING night, the young bride approached her new husband and playfully asked for $20 for their first lovemaking encounter. In his highly aroused state, her husband eagerly agreed.

Thus, it was repeated, every time they made love, throughout their marriage, for more than 30 years. She thought it was fun and exciting; he thought it was a cute way for her to have a little extra spending cash, and afford new clothes and other personal items that she otherwise might not want to buy, thinking the expense was too frivolous.

One day, she arrived at home around 3:00 PM and was surprised not only to find her husband home, but in a very drunken state. During the next few minutes, he explained to her that his employer was going through a process of corporate downsizing, and he had been let go. So, here he was, at the age of 59, without a job. It was unlikely that anyone would hire him at that age, particularly for a position that paid anywhere near what he had been earning before. In other words, they were financially ruined.

Calmly, his wife went upstairs, and returned a few minutes later with a bank statement that showed more than 30 years of steady deposits and compound interest that totaled nearly $1 million. Then she showed him certificates of deposits, issued by the bank, that were worth more than $2 million. She explained that during the more than three decades she'd been "charging" him for sex, she had been buying certificates of deposit from the bank. These holdings had matured and multiplied, and their savings and investments were now worth over $2 million!

Needless to say, her husband was so astounded he could barely speak. The fact that he had been drinking since roughly 11:00 AM didn't help, either. Finally, he found his voice and, with tears in his eyes, blurted out, "Shweetie, if I'd had any idea wh-whaat you were do-ooing with tha' mo-o-ney, I would've givvvenn you *all* of my business!"

Today, she is a wealthy widow. His body was never found.

CHRISTMAS IN HEAVEN

THREE MEN DIED on Christmas Eve and were met by St. Peter at the pearly gates.

"In honor of this holy season," St. Peter said, "here in Heaven we do something special that we don't do at any other time of year. Anyone who dies on Christmas Eve is admitted directly into Heaven, with no further questions asked, provided that he or she died in the possession of something that symbolizes Christmas."

With that, each of the three men began anxiously fumbling through the pockets of their trousers and jackets.

The first man pulled a lighter out of his pants pocket and flicked it on. He said, "This represents a Christmas candle!"

"You may pass into Heaven," said St. Peter.

The second man reached into his jacket pocket and pulled out a set of keys. He shook them and said, "These are the bells of Christmas!"

"You , too, may pass through the pearly gates," said St. Peter.

The third man had searched desperately through his pants pockets and came up with nothing Christmas-like. Finally, he reached into the side pocket of his sports coat and pulled out a pair of women's panties.

St. Peter looked at the man, raised his eyebrows, and said, "And just what do those symbolize?"

The man replied, "They're Carol's!"

LITTLE RED RIDING HOOD

Little Red Riding Hood was skipping down the road, headed into the woods, carrying a picnic basket, on her way to her Grandmother's house.

When she entered the woods, suddenly, she saw a big bad wolf crouched down behind a log.

"My what big eyes you have, Mr. Wolf," she said.

The wolf jumped up and ran away.

Unfazed, Little Red Riding Hood proceeded down the road, but then she saw the big bad wolf again, this time crouched and hiding behind a bush.

"What big ears you have," she said.

Again, the wolf jumped up and ran away.

Little Red Riding Hood continued down the road and through the woods until she saw the big bad wolf again crouching behind a large rock.

"What big teeth you have, Mr. Wolf, she said.

With that, the big bad wolf jumped up and screamed, "Will you knock it off? I'm trying to take a poop!"

PEANUTS

THE TOUR BUS was transporting a group of seniors through Michigan on a Fall Foliage Tour.

As they were rolling down the highway, a sweet little old lady tapped the driver on the shoulder and asked him, "Do you like peanuts?"

The driver said, "Yes, ma'am, I *love* peanuts!"

She said, "Are you allowed to eat them while you drive?"

He said, "I don't see why not!"

So, she leaned over and gave him a handful of peanuts, which he gratefully munched.

Fifteen minutes later, she tapped him on the shoulder again and offered him another handful of peanuts. He happily took them and tossed them into his mouth.

She repeated this generous gesture eight or nine times over the next several miles. "You're sure being generous with your peanuts, ma'am," the driver said. "Are you sure you've got enough for yourselves?"

"Oh, we don't eat the peanuts ourselves," she said. "With our old teeth and dentures, it's impossible for us to chew them."

"Then why do you buy them?" asked the driver.

She replied, "Oh, we just love the *chocolate* around them."

WHERE ARE WE?

JERRY AND ELLEN were on vacation, driving through Louisiana. As they were approaching a town called Natchitoches, a Louisiana city founded in the 1700s and named after an Indian tribe, they began arguing about the pronunciation of the city's name.

Soon, they stopped at a fast food restaurant for lunch and, as they stood at the counter, they decided to get the pronunciation argument settled by a local resident.

Before they placed their order, Jerry leaned over to the girl behind the counter and said, "Could you please settle an argument for us? Would you, please, pronounce where we are, very slowly?"

The girl leaned over the counter and, very distinctly, said, "Burrrr-gerrrr Kiiiing!"

SAY WHAT?

M ARGE AND ROSEMARY were both in their 80s, but age never stopped them from enjoying lunch together at least once a week at a nice restaurant. They had been doing lunch together for years.

At one such lunch, Marge leaned over, looked into Rosemary's ear, and said, "Rosie, did you know you've got a suppository in your left ear?"

Surprised, Rosemary said, "I have?" And she reached up and pulled the suppository out of her ear and stared at it.

After a few minutes, she said, "Marge, I'm glad you saw this thing. Now I think I know where my hearing aid is!"

THE MARRIAGE COUNSELOR

A HUSBAND AND wife went to a marriage counselor after 15 years of marriage.

The counselor asked them what the problem was, and the wife launched into a lengthy tirade, listing virtually every problem, large and small, the couple had ever had in the 15 years they'd been married. She just went on and on for almost 30 minutes.

Finally, the counselor rose up from his chair and walked around to the front of his desk where the husband and wife were seated in guest chairs. He motioned for the wife to stand up, and when she did, he embraced her and kissed her passionately. The stunned woman just sat back down and remained quiet as if in a trance.

The counselor returned to his side of the desk, sat down, turned to the husband, and said, "*That*, sir, is what your wife needs – at least three times a week. Can you do that?"

The husband thought for a moment, and replied, "Well, I can get her here on Mondays and Wednesdays, but Friday is my golf day!"

CHANCE MEETING

WHILE SHOPPING AT the supermarket one Saturday, Kyle noticed a strikingly beautiful blonde in the Produce Department. To his amazement – and gratitude – she looked back at him, then waved and said, "Hello!"

Kyle almost knocked over several displays walking over to her. She looked familiar, but he couldn't quite place why. When he reached her, he said, "Do you know me?"

She replied, "I think you're the father of one of my children."

Now, Kyle was *really* worried. He quickly thought back to the one time he had ever been unfaithful to his wife and said, "Are you the stripper from my brother's bachelor party? The one I had on the pool table with all my buddies watching while your partner, the brunette, whipped my butt with a dog leash?"

Suddenly, the blonde looked very uncomfortable, and said, "No, I'm your son's math teacher!"

THREE OLD GUYS

THREE ELDERLY GENTLEMEN were playing cards in the Activity Room at the Senior Center.

The first old man, a 70-year-old guy, complained, "Every morning, I wake up at 7 o'clock, just to pee! The frustrating thing is, once I'm in the bathroom and wide awake, it takes me 20 minutes before anything happens!"

The second man, who was 80 years old, said, "I've got a similar problem. Every day, I wake up at 8 o'clock for a bowel movement, and it takes 30 minutes before anything happens!"

The third guy, who was 90, said, "I pee like a race horse every morning at 7, and crap like a cow every morning at 8!"

"So, what's your problem?" the other two guys asked.

"I don't wake up 'til 9!"

LUNCHTIME RELIGION

A NEW BUILDING was going up next to a Catholic parish that had a rectory, school, and convent on campus. The construction site was right next door to the convent, and one of the nuns, Sister Rosalita, was becoming quite upset with the coarse language of the workers. So, she decided to spend some time with them to help them change their ways.

Her plan was to sit with some of the workers and talk with them over lunch. So, Sister Rosalita put a sandwich, an apple, and a cupcake for dessert into a brown paper bag. She carried it, along with a bottle of spring water, to the construction site.

Sister Rosalita walked up to the group and, with a big smile, said, "Do you men know Jesus Christ?"

The men all stared at her with a puzzled look. Then, one of the steelworkers looked up to where other men were having lunch while seated on steel beams. He shouted, "Anybody up there know Jesus Christ?"

And one of the steelworkers on the beams yelled down, "Why?"

And the guy yelled up, "'Cuz his wife's here with his lunch!"

PULLING A PRANK ON GRAMPS

THE FAMILY HAD gotten together for the Holidays, and the two teenage boys decided it would be fun to play a prank on Grandpa and Grandma. They ground up a Viagra tablet and dissolved it in one of the several bourbon-and-ginger ale "highballs" Grandpa was enjoying that evening.

A short time after finishing his drink, Gramps, now quite tipsy, excused himself to go to the bathroom. The boys glanced at each other and began giggling.

Soon, Grandpa returned, and the front of his trousers was completely soaked. The boys hadn't expected anything like this, so they asked, "What happened, Gramps?"

He said, "Well, I started to pee, and I noticed what I was holding was so big it couldn't possibly be mine, so I tried to put it back!"

WHAT'S IN A NAME?

THE SCENE: AN upscale cocktail party. A knockout brunette, with green eyes and a stunning figure, scanned the crowd and spotted an attractive man, standing alone with a drink in his hand.

She approached him and said, "Hi, my name is Carmen."

"That's a lovely name," he replied. "Is it a family name?"

"No," she said teasingly, "I gave it to myself. It reflects the things I love the most: cars and men. What's *your* name?"

He said, "B.J. Titsengolf!"

About the Author

Jerry Downey is a veteran advertising Creative Director who has written and produced well over a thousand TV and radio commercials, videos for auto shows and promotional tours, and hundreds of print ads. In addition, Downey spent more than a decade in broadcasting and motion picture publicity.

Jerry and his wife live in Farmington Hills, a suburb of Detroit, Michigan.

www.ingramcontent.com/pod-product-compliance
Lightning Source LLC
Chambersburg PA
CBHW071119170626
46809CB00002B/429